D0451657

Girl, 16

Pants On
Fire

Also by Sue Limb

Girl, 15, Charming but Insane
Girl (Nearly) 16: Absolute Torture

Girl, 16
Pants On Fire

Sue Limb

BLOOMSBURY

First published in Great Britain in 2006 by Bloomsbury Publishing Plc
36 Soho Square, London, W1D 3QY

A CIP catalogue record of this book is available from the British Library

ISBN 0 7475 8216 5
9780747582168

All papers used by Bloomsbury Publishing are natural, recyclable products
made from wood grown in well-managed forests. The manufacturing processes
conform to the environmental regulations of the country of origin.

Typeset by Dorchester Typesetting Group Limited
Printed in Great Britain by Clays Ltd, St Ives plc

1 3 5 7 9 10 8 6 4 2

www.bloomsbury.com
www.SueLimbBooks.co.uk

For Kitty Woodham

1

HONOUR THY FATHER AND THY MOTHER, PARTICULARLY THY FATHER, BECAUSE IF YOU DON'T, NOBODY ELSE WILL

Fred and Jess were sitting under their tree in the park. They'd worked a bit on their latest script, based on the Queen delivering her Christmas message as a rap artist. They'd shared a chocolate ice cream the size of a small piano. A cute dog had visited them and refrained from pooing. Everything was just about as perfect as it could be, except that they had to go back to school tomorrow.

'Did your dad send you a Commandment today?' asked Fred. Jess located it on her mobile and handed it over. Fred read it and laughed. 'It's ironical really,' he said. 'Your dad is just about the least commanding guy I've ever met.'

'True,' said Jess. 'If you were looking for somebody to play God in a Bad Mood, Dad would be the last person you'd choose.'

'You'd probably choose Irritable Powell,' said Fred thoughtfully. Mr Powell, universally known as Irritable, would be their new Head of Year when they got back to school tomorrow. A treat in store.

'I hope I never irritate him,' said Jess. 'His shouting fits can cause structural damage.'

'I wish we were back in St Ives with your dad,' said Fred. 'That was such an amazing trip. I was astounded that he accepted me as your … gentleman companion. And frankly, rather disappointed. I was expecting him to horsewhip me or throw me into the sea.'

'Yeah, it was a brilliant holiday,' sighed Jess. 'I sort of hoped that Dad would be OK about us. But even my mum seemed to tolerate the idea. It was immensely cunning of you to compare her to Jane Austen, you ruthless charmer!'

'We learnt that in our first week at gigolo school,' said Fred. 'It's an appealing career choice, I'm sure you'll agree.'

'Just make sure the next old lady you fascinate is a tad richer than my mum,' said Jess. 'God, it was so embarrassing when Dad and Phil had to pay for the birthday curry!'

Jess's sixteenth birthday had been celebrated in an Indian restaurant the previous week among towering piles of popadoms and seven different vegetable dishes. Her mum, however, had behaved badly by losing her purse and having a panic attack. The purse had turned up later that night, back home under a pile of dirty laundry.

'Thank God Phil had one of those flashy gold credit cards!' said Jess in rapture. 'In fact, he's completely divine. What could be better than a camp stepfather with a boutique and a boat? I can't wait to get back to school tomorrow and boast about my dad being gay.'

Jess sent her dad a text message saying **PICNIC IN THE PARK WITH FRED. WISH YOU WERE HERE. SCHOOL TOMORROW. YOU'LL BE FAMOUS BY LUNCHTIME. OR SHOULD I SAY INFAMOUS?**

'I don't know how to say this,' said Fred suddenly. There was an odd, sad note to his voice. Jess's heart missed a beat. He looked up at her, his head resting on his hand.

'What? *What?*' said Jess. 'You're not ill or something, are you? You're not going to die? I have nothing to wear that would be suitable for your funeral.' Inside, she was suddenly *really worried*.

'You're going to hate me for this,' said Fred.

'I already hate you more than anyone else on earth,' said Jess. 'So go for it! Spill the beans.'

'The thing is,' Fred rolled over on to his back and stared up through the branches of the tree to the sky, 'I have real problems about going back to school.'

'God, don't we all?' said Jess, though really she was looking forward to it. It would be so cool. Her dad was gay, which would enormously increase her prestige. And, even more wonderful, everyone would know she and Fred were together. She was going to be so immensely proud, she might just have to sell their story to the newspapers.

'No, I mean …' Fred hesitated, and rolled over on to his chest. 'I don't mean just the routine back-to-school nausea and boredom stuff. I mean, I have problems, with … you know, our so-called relationship.'

An invisible spear hurtled down through the air and pinned Jess's heart to the earth.

'What do you mean?' She tried for a light-hearted tone but somehow it came out in a desperate gasp, as if she was a fish that had suddenly found itself out of its beloved water and trapped in the horrible dry burning air.

'I'm sorry to be such a prat,' Fred went on, not looking at Jess, but staring instead at the grass just below his face, 'but the thought of everybody at school giving us a hard time ... You know, uh – the ridicule ... the jokes ... Foul! The thought of it makes me want to walk over to the railings over there and hurl my recent lunch into the nettles.'

'Don't be stupid,' said Jess. Her hands had started to shake. 'Nobody'll be even the slightest bit interested.'

'It's just,' said Fred, suddenly taking refuge in a silly posh voice, 'that I've got my reputation to think of, my dear. My identity, you know? I'm the – how can I put it? Eccentric loner. I am historically unable to form relationships. If everybody knows that we're together I shall lose whatever street cred I ever had and be despised as a doting nerd.'

Jess's arteries were now pumping to maximum. Her *Fight or Flight* mechanism had kicked in. How could Fred be saying these horrible, heartless things? Had she never really known him after all? Did he really care more about his so-called glamorous loner's identity than his relationship with her?

Everything glorious that they had shared that summer suddenly took on a sad, doomed kind of air. The fabulous time at the seaside with her dad and Phil and Mum and Granny. She was so proud of Fred, she couldn't wait for everyone at school to know they were together. But it seemed he wasn't proud of her. Oh no. He was *ashamed* of her, apparently.

'Well, I'd hate you to be inconvenienced in any way,' she snapped. 'God forbid that you should be thought a doting nerd. So what is all this? Are you dumping me?'

'Oh no, no, not at all, of course not,' said Fred, avoiding her eye. 'It's just, well, I thought we might just keep it all under wraps, as we used to say in MI5.' He'd put on the posh voice again. Though Jess usually loved all Fred's comedy voices, right now it infuriated her. It was as if he was escaping from her by pretending to be somebody else.

'You know,' Fred went on. 'We could avoid being seen together, except in disguise. Never actually talk, just leave notes in each other's lockers – in code. We could even stage a massive row. Or put out some misinformation – pretend we're deadly enemies.'

Jess could not speak. She could not believe it. She cared more about Fred than anyone else on earth, and he wanted to pretend they were deadly enemies. Her world was shattered. Suddenly she just couldn't bear it any longer. She scrambled to her feet – not elegantly, alas, more like a hippo in haste.

'Why not do the job properly?' she said, struggling

to keep her voice light and ironical. 'Never mind pretending – let's actually *be* deadly enemies. Strange that perfect happiness can give way suddenly to complete hell, but I suppose that's life. Goodbye.'

Fred looked up in alarm. Tears, which Jess had been hoping to keep private, burst suddenly from her eyes. She turned abruptly and marched off.

'Wait! Don't be an idiot!' called Fred. He was getting up. Jess broke into a run. 'Jess! Come back! I was only kidding!' Fred started to chase her.

The moment she heard the words *only kidding*, a kind of explosion happened in Jess's insides. For a moment, she was more *immensely* relieved than she had ever been in her life – not counting the much-postponed comfort stop on the school trip to Stratford-upon-Avon.

But a moment later, she began to doubt it. Only kidding? How could he have made a joke of something so sacred? How could he have upset her so much? She would never speak to him again. She would never even look at him again. Never even refer to him. Never pronounce the word 'Fred', even when discussing Freddie Mercury. Perhaps never even use any word at all beginning with 'F'. Although that might be hard.

And anyway, she didn't believe he *had* been joking.

13

There had been something horribly real about the way he'd confessed his fears. He'd been hesitant and the posh voice hadn't been convincing. If it had really been a joke, Fred would have given a much more polished performance. Well, joke or not: either way, right now she hated him with a bitter, burning passion.

She could hear Fred panting and yelling as he chased her. It wasn't exactly an Olympic event. Overweight girl – slightly overweight girl – wearing new, much-too-tight shoes, chased by bookish boy with long wobbly legs who is intellectually opposed to the whole notion of physical exercise.

Eventually, of course, Fred caught up with her. After all, he was wearing trainers. He grabbed her jacket. It ripped.

'You idiot!' yelled Jess, and turned to face him. Fred grabbed her wrist. His large grey eyes were bigger than ever.

'Stop! Don't be silly!' he panted. 'It was only a joke. I was just kidding.'

'Some joke!' yelled Jess, struggling to get free. 'You dumping me! Big laughs!'

'Of course I'm not dumping you!' said Fred. 'You're the whatyacallit of my life! I worship the pavement outside your house! I would rather walk down the High Street in my boxer shorts than lose you! I'd rather actually *take a dump* on the stage in front of the whole school than dump you!'

Jess closed her mind to all this sordid talk of dumping. She was horribly, insanely furious with him. She felt completely out of control.

'Well, as it happens,' she seethed, 'what you said in jest, I'd been feeling for some time anyway.' Words came tumbling out of her mouth. She hardly even knew what she was saying. All she knew was that she wanted to hurt Fred, to pay him back for the horrible pain that he had caused her. Fred's whole body sort of cringed, and his face crumpled.

'What?' he gasped, grabbing at her again.

'Let me go!' shouted Jess, struggling, hysterical. 'It's over. I've had it up to here with you, and what you said just now is the final insult. Goodbye.'

'I'm sorry!' said Fred. He went down on his knees. 'It was retarded. Forgive me! Set me nine impossible tasks. I'll do them. I'll eat tofu – anything.'

'Excuse me,' said Jess icily. 'I'm going home.' She stepped past him and walked briskly off towards the park gate.

Somehow she expected to hear Fred running up after her again. But he didn't. Jess went through the gate and turned left to go home. No bounding footsteps followed her. She was desperate to turn round and run back to him, or at least look and see what he was doing, but she just couldn't.

Besides, she had a lot of crying to do, once she got home. First of all, she had to cry about Fred saying such cruel things: being ashamed of her. Then she had to cry about the way she'd reacted, making things worse. Last of all – and worst – she had to cry because Fred hadn't followed her begging and pleading to be forgiven, but had just somehow stayed dumbly behind in the park, the fool. How in the world had this awful row just blown up out of nowhere? Were they finished for good, or was it just a row? Either way, she was heartbroken.

Luckily, because Jess had had such a happy summer up till now, her teddy bear Rasputin was divinely dry, absorbent and ready to soak up whole monsoons of crying.

2

THOU SHALT NOT PESTER THY FATHER TO BUY THEE SMALL DOGS

Granny was asleep in front of the TV when Jess got home, so she could run upstairs and sob her heart out unobserved. Eventually Mum came home from a long hard afternoon drooling over plants in the Garden Centre. Some time later, a delicious smell of Mexican food drifted up the stairs.

But Jess couldn't face food. Her heart was broken. Her mum came upstairs to fetch her down to supper, and Jess made up an excuse about having a tummy bug. Mum gave her a very searching look. You could just tell she *knew* it was boy trouble. She was so obviously fighting to stop herself saying, '*See? Men just chew you up and spit you out. Don't say I didn't warn you.*'

Instead she said, 'Well, it's back to school tomorrow, so here's your clean shirt.' Being a mum involved such endless drudgery. Jess was determined she would never have a baby. After this afternoon, she wasn't sure she could handle relationships with the opposite sex. And she didn't like the sound of test tube babies. Jess had always hated science.

Later that evening Jess applied a huge amount of black eye make-up to hide the evidence of crying, and went downstairs to ring Flora, her best friend. Flora was blonde, beautiful and loaded, but she still managed, somehow, to be adorable. She was always particularly good when Jess needed comfort and support. She had a strong motherly streak (unlike Jess's actual mother), always told Jess she looked great, and even enjoyed baking.

Right now Jess was desperate to pour out her troubles and have Flora put it all in perspective. She'd have to ring her on the landline. Flora wasn't allowed to use her mobile at home, because her parents were afraid of brain damage. As Flora always got straight As in every subject, Jess privately thought a little teeny bit of brain damage might have been quite a good thing for Flora, but anyway, the landline offered the chance to chat for hours without charge.

Jess reckoned she wouldn't be overheard because

18

Mum and Granny were watching an archaeological programme called *Time Team*.

'I love this programme because it makes me feel young,' confided Granny. 'Look! An Iron Age skull! I may be over sixty but I'm certainly in better shape than *her*!'

Jess went out to the kitchen, closed the door behind her, and dialled Flora's number. Flora's frightening father answered.

'Barclay!' he barked.

'Er, hello, this is Jess. Could I speak to Flora, please?'

'One moment!' he said, and then Jess heard him say, 'Flora, it's Jess – keep it short. I don't want my evening ruined by teenage cackling.' This was rude, but typical of Mr Barclay, known affectionately to his daughters as 'The Great Dictator'.

'Hi, babe!' said Flora. 'How's everything?'

She sounded on edge. You could tell her parents were listening. This was so frustrating.

'Look, I just wanted to say I'll come round tomorrow morning and we can walk to school together, yeah?' said Jess. She couldn't bear the thought of walking in alone.

'What about Fred?' asked Flora with deadly, cruel accuracy. It was a fair enough question. Jess and Fred had walked to school together for years – long before they had ever become An Item.

'I had a row with Fred today,' said Jess. 'We're not speaking.'

'Oh no! You poor thing!' cried Flora. A horrid, unworthy thought zipped through Jess's mind. Flora had once had a hell of a crush on Fred. Would she now pounce on him like a dog grabbing a fallen biscuit? 'I'm sure it'll all blow over,' Flora went on. 'But yeah, of course, come over tomorrow, OK?'

So next morning, her face pale with sleepless torment (and make-up, to be honest), Jess arrived on Flora's doorstep. Flora gave her a big hug, which did help. Perhaps to show solidarity, Flora was wearing a dull grey jacket and no make-up whatever. Of course, Flora still looked like a goddess, but what was the poor girl to do? She was stuck with Great Beauty. Life was so unfair.

Briefly Jess told Flora how she and Fred had had their row, and Flora said it was horrid of Fred to try and make a joke of something like that, but, hey, wasn't Fred a comedy artist?

'Come on, babe! I'm sure he'll be waiting by the school gates and he'll fall on his knees and beg for forgiveness. You'll be back together by lunchtime, believe me.'

Jess sighed. She certainly hoped so.

'And anyway, there's going to be loads of terrific stuff to do this term,' said Flora. 'You and Fred will do a comedy sketch in the Christmas Show, won't you? I'm sure Mr Fothergill will want you to star in the show. He thinks you're a comedy legend. The Lisa Simpson of Ashcroft School.'

'You're more of a Lisa Simpson,' said Jess. 'I'm an under-achieving female Bart.'

She smiled slightly at the thought of dear, fat, enthusiastic Mr Fothergill. He was Head of English and he had given her so much help and encouragement last term when she had worked on her first piece as a stand-up comedian. In his sweaty way, Mr Fothergill was a little bit of a darling.

'And another thing,' said Flora. 'Mr Fothergill's probably going to be our class tutor this year.'

Jess cheered up quite a bit at this thought. Mr Fothergill would certainly make registration something of a comedy event. And she knew that she and Fred were favourites of his – even though teachers weren't supposed to have favourites. So, if she and Fred could get back together immediately and begin working on a comedy double act with Mr Fothergill's help, life would stop being hell and just might start to feel more heavenly than ever.

The first disappointment was that Fred wasn't waiting at the school gates. Jess felt embarrassed somehow that he wasn't there. As if he didn't care enough about her, or something. Flora knew she was feeling this. Though blonde, she was perceptive.

'He wouldn't want to see you in a public place like this, babe,' she said hastily. 'That was stupid of me. He'll avoid you until he can get you on your own. In a corner of the school field at break. That's where you'll stage your big reconciliation. A secret cuddle under the trees. How romantic!'

Jess managed the ghost of a smile. They entered the bustling throng of the main corridor. Schoolkids everywhere – but no Fred. The bell rang for assembly. They made their way to the school hall.

The head teacher Mrs Tomkins droned on and on about the new term, a new start, new opportunities. But Jess wasn't listening. She was desperately searching through the rows in front. She could easily recognise Fred by the back of his head, but there was no sudden leap of the heart, no joyful recognition. Fred just wasn't there.

Mrs Tomkins began to welcome the new teachers. Jess wondered if Fred was late because something awful had happened to him on his way to school. A bus, out of control? Oh no! Fred was such a dreamer!

Suddenly Mrs Tomkins's voice broke into Jess's anxious hallucinations.

'… Mr Fothergill. We all wish him a speedy recovery. So for this term, Mr Fothergill's place will be taken by Miss Thorn.'

'What?' whispered Jess. 'What's happened to Fothers?'

'He's been hurt in a car accident in Portugal,' Flora whispered back.

Jess's heart lurched in dismay. Poor, dear Mr Fothergill! A car crash! How horrid could today get?

As they filed out to meet their new form tutors, Jess couldn't stop thinking about car crashes.

'Oh my God!' she said. 'I hope the Greased Banana wasn't damaged.' The Greased Banana was Mr Fothergill's little yellow sports car.

'I expect it was a hired car,' said Flora. 'We always hire a car when we go on holiday.'

This was a brief glimpse of how the other half lived. Jess's mum had a very ancient estate car. It was coated with dust and made a ghastly farting noise when it went uphill. Flora's family had a BMW, and hired shiny new cars when they went on holiday. Although, to be fair, they hadn't managed a holiday at all this summer because Flora's mum had broken her leg.

Somehow thinking about accidents made Jess realise she wanted to have a pee. The loos were up ahead.

'Come on,' said Flora. 'We'll be late.'

'Just a min,' said Jess. 'I want to go to the loo.'

'I'll go ahead, then,' said Flora. 'Don't worry, I'll tell them you're here.'

Flora had a horror of being late for anything. It was her dad's influence. Jess wandered into the girls' loos. She was glad her dad was absent and fabulously gay rather than a tyrant like Flora's, giving her a hard time over phone calls and inspecting her bedroom for tidiness every day.

Jess was still looking forward to revealing her dad's stylish homosexuality to a crowd of amazed friends – at lunchtime, maybe. It was some comfort, despite the row with Fred, to know that she had some gold-star gossip up her sleeve.

The loos were deserted. Everyone else was at registration. After going to the loo, Jess decided she would design herself a new pair of eyebrows. She wanted to wow everyone with her ability to project wit and irony through make-up. And if it made Fred realise she was the catch of the century, even better.

Ten minutes later, she was done. The eyebrows were magnificent. She carried them reverently out of the loos and along the corridor, and planned to open the classroom door just slightly, and sort of stick her head round the corner with a wacky expression. And say, in Lisa Simpson's voice, 'Is this the right class? I'm new! My name's Arabella Smeller and I've just blown in from Acne, Ohio.'

She opened the door just slightly as planned, but there was a strange sound inside. The sound of silence. Her class had never, ever sounded like that. There should surely have been chatting, even low-key. There should surely be a bit of comfortable, relaxed bitching. But instead there was silence.

Jess pushed the door open and ventured in. She was instantly face to face with a terrifying woman. She had straight black hair cut in a severe bob. Her eyebrows were a lot more cruel than Jess's. And she was wearing an extremely smart Armani-type suit, with a collar and old-fashioned tie. Her lipstick was very red. And her eyes were extremely hostile.

'You're late!' she observed coldly. 'This is a poor start. What's your name?'

'Arabella Smeller,' faltered Jess, though she couldn't quite manage the accent. It seemed unlikely that she could dissolve the atmosphere with a mild joke or two. Her classmates were all sitting very still in their places. Nobody even smiled. Her big comedy entrance had fallen totally flat.

'I'm Miss Thorn,' said the dragon. 'I assume you're Jess Jordan. I've just marked you as absent, despite your friend's assurances you were here. You have to be in this room by 8.45, otherwise you are deemed late or absent. And no amount of lame excuses or attempts to be humorous will wash with me. Is that clear?'

'Ah,' said Jess, mortified that she had ever thought the name Arabella Smeller had comic potential. 'Sorry.' She was beginning to feel really cross with Mr Fothergill for being in a car crash. He had let them down badly. Now they had to endure this gorgon.

'Go and sit down,' said Miss Thorn coldly.

Jess gave a sober little nod, looked at the floor, and raised her magnificent eyebrows just slightly. Now was the moment when she would look up and catch Fred's eye, as she walked to her seat beside Flora. OK, so her arrival hadn't been the hilarious triumph she had planned. But she felt that at least she had stood her ground, and Fred would be impressed.

But what was this? Horror! Fred was nowhere to be seen.

3

THOU SHALT NOT WRITE RUDE WORDS ON THE WALLS OF PUBLIC LOOS

After registration, they had double maths. Being a bit of a dumbo when it came to figures, Jess was in a very basic maths set called G5. Flora, of course, was in the top set. They agreed to meet at mid-morning break and share a chocolate milkshake from the school tuck shop before embarking on a severe diet involving only protein.

'And it's got to be protein that's still alive,' said Jess. 'Obviously. We've got to think, snake.'

'What, eat snakes?' screamed Flora, as they walked through the sunlit quad.

'No, you idiot, we've got to *be* snakes,' said Jess. 'Snakes always eat living protein, and you can see how it pays off. Did you ever see a snake with cellulite?'

Flora grinned, and they parted: Flora to join the eggheads in Maths G1 and Jess to trudge off to a dark, dank, slimy corner of the school where the sun never shone: Where The Dumb Things Are. The minute she was alone again, her heart sank. She could actually feel it throbbing away down in her pelvis, like a bad-tempered baby clamouring to be born.

So much bad stuff happening today! Fred sulking so much he was invisible, poor old Fothergill injured in an accident, and this new teacher who looked as if she could eat a whole barbecue complete with red-hot coals without flinching. For an instant Jess was tempted to send Fred a text message asking him where he was and imploring him to come to school and rescue her from the dragon that was Miss Thorn, but the bell rang and Jess was already late.

Ms Burton, the maths teacher, had gone blonde, but Jess still couldn't dredge up any interest in algebra. Although she did have a great commercial idea for a bra covered with algebraic formulae called an Alge-bra. Maybe she would become a great clothing design entrepreneur and make a million before she was twenty-five. It would console her slightly for the loss of Fred's love. She might even get herself an Armani suit and a fierce haircut like Miss Thorn's.

No, it wouldn't console her for the loss of Fred's

love. Nothing would. Jess began to feel that life would not be possible beyond 11am unless a) she heard from Fred or b) she devoured a chocolate bar.

Jess had an idea for a bra that was dark brown and smelt of chocolate. It was called a Chocolate Brar. She designed a bra that was striped, black and white. It was called a Ze-bra. She conjured up the possibility of a snakeskin bra called a Co-bra. She roughed out a sketch of a bra fitted with five lighted candles, called a Candela-bra.

No, that last idea was rubbish. One wouldn't wish one's lingerie to be a fire risk. Still, designing joke lingerie did at least get her through double maths without losing the will to live. Although, to be honest, it was flickering.

At last the bell rang, and Jess regained the divine freedom of the corridor. Ben Jones strolled up. At last, a moment of pleasure. Jess grinned. Ben looked more handsome than ever. He looked, right now, just like David Beckham's younger brother. A few months ago Jess had had a mega-crush on Ben. But gradually it had worn off, and once Fred had admitted that he wouldn't mind going out with her, just on a trial (money back if not delighted) – well, that had been the end of all Jess's interest in Ben. Except as a very dear friend, of course.

'Hi, Jess!' Ben grinned, with his usual immensely slow charm. 'How was your, um – holiday 'n' stuff?'

'Terrific,' said Jess. She was so tempted to send Fred a text. But shouldn't Fred be sending *her* a text? After all, he was the one who had started all this, with his stupid idea about pretending to be deadly enemies.

'How's Fred?' said Ben, leaning his designer bum on the nearby wall. At the mention of Fred's name, Jess felt a stabbing pain in her heart. She blushed.

'We had a row,' she said. 'We're not speaking. He's not even here today.'

'A row?' Ben looked surprised. 'What about? – Sorry, none of my – uh, business, but …'

'He didn't want people to know about us,' said Jess. 'Basically I think he's ashamed of me.'

Ben's eyes widened. They were somehow even bluer than last year. Perhaps he had coloured contact lenses and had changed the shade from Mediterranean to Caribbean Blue.

'Harsh,' he murmured. 'Where you going now?'

'I was going to meet Flora at the tuck shop,' said Jess. 'You know the saying? Miserable women console themselves with food.'

'Mind if I – tag along?' asked Ben. 'I'll buy you a snack. What do you fancy? Or have you – you know,

30

kind of – lost your appetite?'

'Certainly not!' said Jess, as they set off for the tuck shop. 'I'd never let a mere man put me off my grub.'

'Glad to hear it,' said Ben. 'I hear they've got guacamole-flavour crisps in now. Fancy ... uh, sharing a packet?'

'Sure,' said Jess. It was always nice to be with Ben – now that she'd got over her crush, she appreciated his kindness. And though he always described himself as a complete dumbo, she had the feeling that, deep down, he was quite sensitive, really. For a male person, anyway.

They reached the tuck shop, but Flora wasn't there. Ben treated Jess to a bag of the new crisps and a Coke. Then Jess treated Ben to a chocolate bar and a fruit smoothie. They finished their guzzling with a chocolate milkshake. And then, for Jess, there was the challenge of not burping raucously in front of Ben.

OK, she hadn't got a crush on him any more, but a girl doesn't want to open her mouth in public and emit a clap of thunder. (Though in private or with other girls, of course, it would be a great way to while away a rainy afternoon.)

Ben was talking about football practice (he was captain of the team) and Jess was half-listening and half-worrying about Fred. Where on earth was he? Was he ill? Had he been run over? Should she text him at lunchtime or wait till she got home? Should she call in at his house on the way back tonight?

'If ...' Ben was frowning slightly, as if struggling with an immensely difficult concept. Jess's attention was distracted, for a moment, from thoughts of Fred. Ben always did find it hard to put things into words, and right now it seemed he needed access to her verbal skills.

'If ... I don't know, you might not – but if you did ...'

'What?' said Jess, but it came out sort of sharp and aggressive. 'What?' she added, more softly and without so much spit.

'I just wondered ...' Ben burbled on. He rubbed his divine cheek with his suntanned hand. Now that she wasn't mad about him, Jess could appreciate his good looks in the same way that one might admire, say, a beautiful beach. Not that she was tempted to run barefoot across him, no no –

'I just wondered if you'd like to come and watch football practice tonight,' said Ben.

Jess was puzzled. Ben had never asked her to football practice before. She felt football was a game best left to baboons and other slightly less evolved members of the Great Apes.

'Might cheer you up, sort of thing,' said Ben. 'If you're upset about Fred and stuff. Come and watch us lunatics training. Should be a laugh. You could, well – help me choose the team.'

'Help you choose?' Jess was intrigued by this idea. Perhaps a career as a football manager might prove more lucrative – and more exciting – than designing lingerie or being a stand-up comedian.

'Yeah, I have to – y'know, discuss it with Mr Monroe tomorrow,' said Ben. 'There's about twenty guys and we've gotta, uh, get it down to eleven by Saturday.'

Dear, kind Ben! So worried that she was feeling blue that he'd invited her to a football practice of all things! Not realising that, for her, this would only add to her torture! Jess forced herself into a really bright, tight smile. It felt a size too small, but she persevered.

'Oh Ben, thanks so much – maybe some other time, yeah? Only I've got such heaps to do this evening, stuff I've been putting off for ages. My mum will kill me if I'm not home straight after school,' said Jess.

Ben's sky-blue eyes were fixed intently on her. For a moment, when he registered the fact that she had declined his invitation, it was as if a cloud had briefly covered the sky. It was only a split second, the merest moment, but somehow it was disturbing. Oh God! She'd hurt his feelings!

'OK, cool,' said Ben quickly. 'Gotta go now – geography, yeah? See you!' He gave her a brief nod, turned and strolled off down the corridor. Jess watched him go. A couple of girls passed him, and she saw the look of adoration that filled their eyes, and the crazy giggles of excitement which overwhelmed them as he passed.

A few months ago, she'd been like that. And now, here she was turning down his invitation to watch football practice. A year ago, she would have dug an underground tunnel from her home to the sports field just to catch a glimpse of his divine white boots. Now ... now things were so different.

She'd have to be really friendly and appreciative to Ben next time they met. Despite being the school love god, he seemed strangely vulnerable sometimes. He'd told Jess, last term, that he didn't want a girl-friend – didn't feel able to cope with the idea. Perhaps it was because so many girls were throwing themselves at him. What a strange life it must be, as a sex symbol.

Jess didn't have time to think about it now though.

She just had to get back to worrying about Fred. Plus she was already late for English. Oh God! It would be Miss Thorn again! Jess broke into a run, and raced towards the English department. And where on earth was Flora? Had a first day of term ever been so stressful?

4

THOU SHALT NOT
SHAVE THY EYEBROWS,
NEITHER THY ARMS:
IT IS AN
ABOMINATION

Jess raced to Room 10, where they always used to have English last year. There was a sign on the door. *Please go to Room 16.* Oh, Lawdy, Lawdy! Jess whirled round and hurtled off in the opposite direction.

Room 16 was up two flights of stairs. Jess charged up them, aware that all around her the school had settled down quietly. She was mega-late for Miss Thorn *again*. And in the privacy of her gut, the crisps, chocolate bar and fruit smoothie were kind of jostling up together with the Coke in a way which was far from pleasant. Here was Room 16! Jess barged in, and stood panting in front of Miss Thorn.

The room was icy and silent again. Miss Thorn's

eyes glittered with annoyance.

'Late again, I see,' she observed sourly. Jess's mind whirled. She had to conjure up a fabulous excuse. She would play the period pain card. Jess opened her mouth to begin her tragic account of agonising cramps, but no words came out – only a huge, deafening burp:

'Waaaaaaarp!'

Miss Thorn's eyes flared with indignation.

'I'm so sorry!' stammered Jess. 'I've got a bit of a tummy upset!'

'Is that why your face is covered with chocolate?' enquired Miss Thorn acidly.

Hastily Jess wiped her face with her hand. There was indeed chocolate – on her fingers, now. Ben should have told her, the idiot.

'I'm giving you a yellow card,' said Miss Thorn coldly. Jess's mind whirled. A yellow card? What was that, again? It sounded quite nice. Yellow was a cheerful colour, after all.

'I see myself as a kind of football referee,' explained Miss Thorn. 'For bad behaviour, you get a yellow card. That means you're on a warning. One more offence and you get a red card. That means a trip to the Head of Year. Plus you lose some very important privileges.'

Jess nodded and tried to look humble. She didn't want to be sent to Irritable Powell. When he shouted, all the windows in the school vibrated.

'I'm really sorry,' said Jess, looking at the floor.

'Go and sit down,' said Miss Thorn, turning back to the blackboard. Jess fled to her place next to Flora. Miss Thorn was writing something on the board.

'Where were you at break?' whispered Jess. Miss Thorn whirled round.

'Quiet!' she snapped. Jess tried to look as though she had no desire to speak ever again, and shuffled her feet about as if it might have been her feet that had done the whispering.

Flora wrote something on the cover of her rough book. *I was talking to Miss Thorn*, it said. *There isn't going to be a Christmas Show this term.*

'What?' gasped Jess aloud. Miss Thorn turned round again.

'Jess Jordan, come down here and sit at the front.'

Jess got up and picked up her things, trying not to look too satirically weary, though she was so, so tempted just to blow her whole school career and yell, *Kiss my AAAAARSE!*

However, the thought of Mr Powell's terrible roaring voice and awful, hairy quivering nostrils was too much, so she sort of slunk down to the front and slid into one of the many empty seats down there. Nobody had wanted to be anywhere near Miss Thorn.

Down here at the front, you could even smell her perfume. It was quite classy in a cool kind of way, Ralph Lauren or something. Her own mum never used classy, cool perfumes. She couldn't afford them. She used those tiny bottles of essential oils. It was usually coconut. And she hardly ever used scent at all, so the bottles of coconut oil were, to be honest, a bit past their smear-by date. So most of the time Jess's mum smelt a bit like a rather rancid tropical lagoon.

'Right,' said the fragrant but frightening Miss Thorn. 'Your essay title is on the board. I want absolute silence.'

The title was *My Family*. Jess thought this was rather impertinent. What business was it of Miss Thorn's? Why should she tell her anything at all about her family? After all, Miss Thorn hadn't confided any details of *her* home life. If indeed she had a home life. Jess was beginning to think that, when she went home, Miss Thorn climbed inside a cast-iron coffin and was fed intravenously with the blood and milk of Transylvanian she-wolves.

Jess was deeply bored by the idea of writing about her family. Then suddenly she had a thought. If she created a really tragic family history, Miss Thorn might stop being irritated with her and start to feel pity and admiration. OK then, she would lay it on extra-thick.

I don't really like talking about my family, she began, trying to make her handwriting brave and disadvantaged. It's a sensitive issue. My dad grew up in total poverty. His parents couldn't afford proper food and once they even had to make a stew out of their own dog, Bruno. Luckily Bruno was a Newfoundland. If he'd been a Chihuahua, Dad probably wouldn't have survived into adulthood.

A poor diet as a child meant that Dad grew up over-weight, with grey, pasty skin and chronic bad breath. (Actually Jess's dad was tall, fair and quite handsome, with breath as sweet as a spring day.) Dad's breath is really embarrassing. We were at the cinema one day and the man sitting in front of us turned to his wife and said, 'I can smell gas!'

Because of his troubled childhood, Dad has phobias. He's afraid of dogs (it's the guilt about eating Bruno). He'll cross the street to avoid a dog, but it's worse than that – he'll even cross the street to avoid a person who looks like a dog.

He's not just afraid of big, horrible things like wars and earthquakes, he's afraid that I, his only child, am in danger from household objects.

'Don't go near the microwave!' he yells, even when it's off. 'Don't sit too near the TV! Rays come out of it!' And food is a minefield. 'Don't eat burgers!' he begs me. 'They can kill you in five different ways!'

When I was little and I'd gone to bed, he would wake me up every twenty minutes to make sure I was still alive.

Dad is always imagining he's ill. I once caught him in the bathroom, trying to look up his nose with Mum's make-up mirror.

'Sorry, love,' he said. 'Just hunting for polyps.' I ran screaming from the house, and shortly afterwards my parents' marriage ended.

Miss Thorn would surely feel a pang of sympathy on reading this. And because Dad lived too far away to attend parents' evenings, Miss Thorn would never know that, though slightly nervous about his health, Jess's dad wasn't a bad old stick, really.

Now, what could Jess say about her mum? She thought for a minute. It would have to be subtle, because there was always a chance that Miss Thorn might meet her mum one day. Jess's mother was always first in the queue at parents' evenings, and even made horrid notes in an exercise book, under-lining phrases such as 'Check on <u>homework</u> – and make sure Jess has not <u>forged my signature</u> in homework record book'.

My mother appears normal, **wrote Jess.** But her mild manner hides a ferocious temper. Anything can set her off. Thursday is my usual day for a beating. She has thrashed me with a whole range of household objects, including, on one occasion, a whole frozen haddock.

(In fact Jess's mum was a pacifist who worked as a librarian, and was so opposed to violence she even found it hard to set mousetraps or swat flies. In the summer she usually just opened windows and implored the wasps to leave.)

When not in a rage, my mum is more tolerable. But she is frighteningly absent-minded. Her life revolves around gardening and books. Cooking for me, her beloved daughter, is not a priority. Whilst halfway through preparing supper recently, Mum rushed out into the garden because she'd noticed that one of her shrubs was looking a bit sickly. I smelt something odd and came downstairs to the kitchen, where I found a large steak in the bookcase and 'The Secret Diary of Adrian Mole' frying gently with onions and garlic.

But my granny's the really dangerous one, **Jess finished with a flourish.** She's obsessed with murder. In fact, I sometimes think she's planning one. It's a bit like living with a twisted version of Miss Marple, where the old lady's not the sleuth, she's the homicidal maniac just waiting to strike.

The bell went, and Jess sat back with a satisfied sigh. She looked up, and found Miss Thorn's strange piercing eyes fixed on her.

'Place your essays on my desk as you go out,' said Miss Thorn. 'Except for you, Jess Jordan. You can stay behind for a moment. I'll read yours *now*.'

5

THOU SHALT NOT DISS
THE LORD THY DAD
THAT IS IN CORNWALL,
BUT WORSHIP HIM
ALWAYS

Miss Thorn's eyes ran swiftly through Jess's comic masterpiece, her face betraying no reaction whatever. After she had read it, she handed it back with delicate disdain, as if it was a prawn sandwich that had gone off.

'One of the things we have to learn as we grow up,' said Miss Thorn in a preachy voice, 'is that comedy is not always appropriate.'

Damn! thought Jess. *I must have overdone the tragedy and toppled over into the farcical.* She'd sort of known her essay was a bit far-fetched, but she hadn't been able to resist the temptation.

'I want you to rewrite this by tomorrow morning,'

Miss Thorn went on. Standing up close like this, Jess could see that Miss Thorn had designed her eyebrows to be deliberately frightening. Although she already hated her deeply, she had to admire her skill with cosmetics.

'All I want is a simple description of your actual family, not all this nonsense.' Miss Thorn tossed a kind of sneering glance at Jess's work. Jess decided not to get into an argument. There was something else on her mind.

'OK. Er, is it true that we're not having a Christmas Show this year?' she asked, trying not to sound too indignant.

'We *are* having a Christmas Show,' said Miss Thorn. '*Twelfth Night*.'

'I meant a Revue like we normally have,' said Jess. 'With sketches and songs and stuff.'

'No,' said Miss Thorn. '*Twelfth Night* is Mr Fothergill's favourite play, apparently, and he's hoping to be well enough by then to come and see it. And Shakespeare actually wrote it to be performed at Christmas.'

'We did *Twelfth Night* with Mr Fothergill all last term,' said Jess. 'I expect he's bored to death with it.'

'There's no such thing as being bored to death with Shakespeare,' said Miss Thorn. 'Except, possibly, for the very immature.'

Jess decided to ignore this insult. She would have her revenge later.

'Ah well,' she said, beginning to think about going, 'maybe I should audition for it.'

'Yes, why not?' said Miss Thorn. 'The auditions are every lunchtime this week – starting tomorrow.'

Jess quite fancied the lead role: Viola. She got shipwrecked, dressed as a boy, was pursued by a lovesick countess and got involved in fights. The girl had what you could call a lifestyle.

'Viola seems kind of a fun part,' said Jess.

'Oh, I don't see you as Viola,' said Miss Thorn. 'You're a bit too short. But we might find something for you – a sailor, perhaps. Or a messenger.'

Jess managed, with a supreme burst of self-control, not to hit Miss Thorn smack in the mouth. Too *short*?

Jess gave what she hoped was a sarcastic shrug, and walked out. But all the way down the corridor she was seething. Too short? Too *short*? How dare the icy bitch make wounding personal remarks? Just because she was so damned tall herself! *Let's hope one day some obliging dog will mistake her for a lamp post and do the honours*, thought Jess. Anyway, it made sense for Viola to be short – because if she was a tall sort of 'boy', her voice would have broken, wouldn't it?

And speaking of tall boys whose voices had broken, where was Fred? If only they hadn't had that stupid row in the park, she could have texted him right now. But if she texted him, it would look as if she was apologising. Jess knew she'd been totally out of control when she'd told Fred to get lost, and had stormed off. She would apologise about that one day. But Fred had started the whole thing off. He was the one who should be apologising! Maybe Miss Thorn was right after all about one thing. Maybe there were times when comedy was not appropriate.

What a dire day this was turning out to be. Perhaps Mercury was retrograde or something. Jess decided her best plan was just to keep out of trouble and try and get through the day minute by minute. On the way home she could decide whether to drop in at Fred's or not.

'I think I might audition for *Twelfth Night*,' said Flora at lunch. Jess was tucking into a pizza, even though she had eaten about 3,000 calories at mid-morning break. Flora was picking daintily at a Caesar salad – and leaving the croutons on the side of her plate.

'I wouldn't audition for that woman!' said Jess. 'Not in a million years. It's so harsh that we can't have a Christmas Show. Fred and I had got so many ideas for sketches.'

'Oh, go on, Jess, please! Let's audition together,' pleaded Flora. 'It would be so cool if we could both be in it.'

'Forget it,' growled Jess, gnawing at the bald bits round the edge of the pizza. 'As far as I'm concerned, that would be sleeping with the enemy.'

Flora shrugged, and shook her head, and looked sadly away. She always did this when they disagreed about something. Jess preferred a glorious head-to-head blazing row, but Flora's family never had rows and Flora just didn't know how to begin. It was quite frustrating, really.

The rest of the afternoon passed in a dull blur, and when the bell rang for end of school Flora and Jess met by the drinks machine.

'I'm going to the music department,' said Flora. 'I want to book my clarinet lessons. Come with me? Then we can walk home.'

'I can't, sorry,' said Jess. 'I'm going to call in on Fred. I've got to sort out this stupid mess we've got ourselves into.'

'Oh right, well, good luck. Hope it all works out OK,' said Flora. 'Give me a ring tonight and tell me how it went. Yeah?'

Jess nodded, and strolled off. She wasn't surprised to find it was raining and blowing a gale. Just her luck. She hesitated by the school gates and got out her umbrella, but the damn thing kept flapping about as if it was alive.

'Hi,' said a voice. 'Want a hand?'

Jess squinted through the rain. It was Ben Jones. He took her umbrella and held it above her, rather like a courteous fellow in a 1940s musical.

'I thought you had football practice?' she said.

'Rained off,' said Ben. Jess felt like an idiot.

'How very delightful to have a gentleman carry my umbrella!' she said in a posh old-fashioned voice. 'Perhaps chivalry is not dead after all!'

Ben laughed. They set off down the road. It's hard to walk under an umbrella with somebody without sort of snuggling up to them in a way, and you feel kind of private under an umbrella, too. A few months ago, Jess would have fainted with joy at the thought of sharing such a romantic experience with Ben Jones.

'I'll see you to your – er, place, if you like,' he said. 'Nothing else to do.'

'That was not quite so chivalrous, Benjamin!' said Jess. Secretly she was abandoning her plan to go to Fred's. She could hardly turn up at his house with

Ben Jones being chivalrous under an umbrella. She felt relieved in a way. She wasn't looking forward to having an awkward and embarrassing scene with Fred. Although until they did sort things out, she knew there would be a heavy weight somewhere in her insides.

They came to the Dolphin Café. A delicious smell of doughnuts drifted out.

Jess's tummy rumbled, rather like a distant roll of thunder.

'Oh my God!' she said. 'I have to have a doughnut!'

'I thought you were in a hurry to get home tonight?' said Ben.

'It's OK – just a quick doughnut and a Coke,' said Jess. 'You're my partner in binge eating, you've got to keep me company. You don't have to actually have anything yourself if you're in training or something.'

They went inside. The café was kind of steamy and cosy. There was a tiny table in a corner by the till. They grabbed it and immediately got stuck into an apple doughnut each.

'Not on some kind of athlete's diet, then?' said Jess. 'I would have thought you had to eat steak and raw eggs all the time. Call yourself a footballer!'

'No, I'm just an, er … sugar junkie,' said Ben. 'I

live on chocolate brownies at home.'

'Nibbling away at cakes all day, and calling off your football practice just because it's raining!' grinned Jess. She put on her old-fashioned 1940s film voice again. 'In my day young men were *real* men. They had fabulous muscles, and divine moustaches lightly dressed with mayonnaise!'

Ben laughed, and finished his doughnut. 'Yeah, well …' he said. Jess waited for him to complete his observation. But it seemed he had.

'You guys are just so limp-wristed!' she said. 'I bet I'm stronger than you anyway.'

'Oh yeah? How about a bit of arm wrestling, then?' suggested Ben.

They clasped hands and anchored their elbows to the table. Just for a split second, at the back of her mind, Jess realised that this was the first time she had held hands with Ben Jones. Although it didn't mean anything, of course. His hand was rather nice – warm, but not sweaty, and big. And strong. Ben forced her hand down with stunning speed. It was humiliating, but kind of wonderful as well.

'Best of three!' said Jess. This time she gritted her teeth and put up one hell of a struggle, but eventually Ben won that one, too.

'Best of five!' demanded Jess. She was determined

to prove she was as strong as he was. They clasped hands again.

Then Jess became aware that somebody was standing by their table. A green raincoat was too close to ignore. Jess looked up, her hand still firmly locked into Ben's.

Dear God in heaven! It was Fred's *mum*! This was the worst moment of Jess's life so far.

6

THOU SHALT NOT WISH ANY OTHER MAN WAS YOUR DAD: YEA, NOT EVEN KEVIN COSTNER

'Mrs Parsons!' squeaked Jess, and struggled to her feet, hastily letting go of Ben's hand. She felt a huge blush sweep up from her toes and break out across her face. Fred's mum smiled, but there was something about her smile which was less than divine.

'Hello, Jess. Wet, isn't it? We just came in to shelter from the rain – so we thought we'd award ourselves a cup of tea.'

Another middle-aged woman, evidently Mrs Parsons's friend, was standing nearby carrying a tray.

'Yeah, we did too,' said Jess. Fred's mum looked down at Ben and smiled at him, but there was just a hint of reserve about it, as if she somehow suspected he was not worthy to lick the feet of her beloved son Fred.

'This is Ben Jones,' said Jess, breaking into a sweat. 'Mrs Parsons is Fred's mum.'

'Hi,' said Ben, nodding and smiling. Then he scrambled to his feet, as if realising he ought to make more of an effort to be polite. 'Sorry. Yeah.' He shook hands with her, awkwardly. It wasn't much help. Ben could have represented his country at arm-wrestling, but when it came to conversation, he really needed a personal coach just to get off the starting blocks.

'Ben's the captain of the football team,' said Jess. 'Ashcroft School's answer to David Beckham – only without the sex appeal.'

Oh my God! Why in the world had she said *that*? She blushed anew. To her horror, Ben also blushed. Even Mrs Parsons turned a little pink. Jess had to change the subject, double quick. She must say something – preferably a remark which did not insult anyone else in the café.

'I was just coming round to your house, actually,' said Jess. 'To see how Fred is. Has he got a tummy bug or something?'

Mrs Parsons frowned.

'A … tummy bug?' she faltered. 'Why?'

'I thought he must be ill,' said Jess. 'Because he wasn't at school.'

'He wasn't at school?' Mrs Parsons's eyes widened with alarm and just a tiny dash of outrage. 'Well, he certainly left for school this morning, at the usual time, in his school clothes.'

'Oh no!' exclaimed Jess. 'Well, he didn't turn up.'

They all stood in silence for a while, thinking about the awful implications. Had Fred been murdered? Had he disappeared, leaving his clothes neatly folded on a bridge or the bank of a canal? Jess's insides turned somersaults, and Mrs Parsons went pale and started to bite her fingernails: never attractive in the middle-aged, and always a sign of parental meltdown.

'Oh dear,' said Mrs Parsons. 'Oh dear. What on earth can have happened? I think I'd better nip back home and see if he's there. I'm so sorry, Margaret.' She turned to her friend and exchanged some angsty murmurs, and then, after a few more *oh dears*, she departed.

Jess and Ben sat down again. Jess felt completely limp with embarrassment and panic. In a half-hearted kind of way, she had been enjoying the arm-wrestling with Ben, but now she knew Fred had not been at home all day, she felt deeply scared.

'What a nightmare,' she whispered. Thank goodness she had already finished her doughnut, because right now she felt so upset she might not eat again for a whole year.

'Fred'll be OK: don't worry,' said Ben.

'Yeah ... yeah, of course.' Jess tried desperately hard to get back into her carefree mood. 'I'm sorry I said you were like David Beckham only without the sex appeal. It was supposed to be a sort of stupid joke.'

Ben smiled, and looked down at the table. He moved a few grains of sugar around with his finger, and his cheeks went rather pink again. How much more blushing could one café accommodate? The windows were already totally steamed up.

'Beckham?' said Ben, and then suddenly raised his eyes to hers in a flash of blue. 'No way. Mackenzie says I look like a – uh – startled meercat.'

Mackenzie was Ben's best mate, and, in Jess's opinion, resembled a bad-tempered Hobbit. He was hardly in a position to diss Ben's looks. Ben was, after all, the nearest thing to a love god at Ashcroft School.

'No, no,' said Jess, getting flustered. She did not want to be having this conversation. She did not want to have to dig herself out of another deep hole. It had been bad enough just now, talking to Fred's mum.

She was conversationally exhausted. With a huge effort, she switched back into the posh 1940s film star voice she'd been playing about with earlier.

'You are, of course, famous among all the gentlemen of my acquaintance for your stunning good looks and stylish trainers. Every girl in the school fancies you, all the gay boys in the school fancy you – possibly even small dogs who pass you in the street fancy you.'

Ben sighed, stared into her eyes, shook his head, and looked away. Jess felt that her huge efforts at 1940s screenplay dialogue had fallen rather flat. Then, suddenly, Ben had an idea.

'Shouldn't you, like, send Fred a text to warn him that his mum knows?' he suggested.

'Oh my God! Yes! Brilliant! Brilliant! You're really brilliant, Ben!' said Jess, and got out her mobile. It was the perfect excuse to get in touch with Fred – nothing personal, just a warning.

Jess hesitated. She was so tempted to apologise or to demand an apology, to make up something funny about where he might possibly have been today, to whizz him a few favourite insults or accuse him of nameless crimes, but it really wasn't the moment. So she simply said JUST MET YOUR MUM IN THE CAFÉ SO SHE KNOWS YOU WERE ABSENT TODAY. SHE'S ON HER WAY

HOME RIGHT NOW. SORRY. JUST WANTED TO WARN YOU. JESS.

'I think I'd better go,' said Jess. She felt restless. She didn't really want to walk home with Ben. She wanted to be alone. Hastily she gulped down the last of her Coke. Ben watched her and sort of rubbed his face in a sleepy way, as if auditioning for a disposable razor ad.

'I think I'll stay here for a bit,' he said. 'Got to try and work out who should be in the team. Have a think.'

'Right,' said Jess, getting up. She wasn't sure if Ben just happened to have done the right thing, or whether he was being really sensitive and considerate. Either way it suited her. She grabbed her bag, said goodbye to Ben in as friendly but distant a way as possible, and squeezed past several other tables to the door.

A squall of rain hit Jess in the face. What a nightmare this day had been. No Fred, Mr Fothergill hurt in a car crash, his place taken by a sadistic she-devil from hell who said Jess was *too short* to play Viola, the cow! And then Flora saying she was going to audition anyway, the treacherous bitch! And then Fred's mum catching her apparently *holding hands* with Ben Jones in the Dolphin Café! And then Jess saying all those awful, awful, cringe-making things that would stay with her for the rest of her life!

And to cap it all the discovery that Fred wasn't ill after all – that he'd just been mysteriously elsewhere! How dare he cut school without her! And where the hell had he been all day? With somebody? Who?? One thing was certain. This was so *not* the moment to drop round at Fred's and sort things out with him. She had never been so exhausted in her life.

Nightmare, nightmare, nightmare! Jess started to run. She was just desperate to get home and collapse in a heap on the sofa, and receive a lot of fuss and attention. Granny was the one person in the world who always had time for her – except her teddy bear Rasputin, of course. Dear Granny!

As she turned into her street, Jess had a sudden ghastly hallucination that, to crown this most awful of days, Granny would be stretched out on her favourite Lake District rug, as dead as a plank and twice as stiff. *Oh Granny! Granny! Granny! Don't be dead! Please God, let my grandmother live!* she prayed feverishly as she hurtled down the last hundred yards and up her own dear, welcoming path.

Damn it! She couldn't find her key. She must have left it behind. She rang the doorbell, and crouched down and peeped through the letterbox into the hall.

The sitting room door opened, and the darling old soul came waddling out to let Jess in.

'Hi, Granny!' yelled Jess. 'It's only me! I've just had the worst day ever and I'm desperately in need of some TLC! So stand and deliver!'

Jess stood up, the door opened, and she fell into Granny's arms. But there was something odd about Granny. She was definitely alive – no worries on that score – but she looked a bit kind of embarrassed and formal.

'What?' said Jess. 'What is it?'

Granny cleared her throat and looked confidential.

'We've got a visitor,' she said quietly. 'And he's Japanese.'

'You're kidding!' Jess could simply not believe it.

'He's in the sitting room, dear, and he's been here for forty minutes already, and still your mum hasn't come home,' said Granny, looking rather tired and, to be honest, majorly pissed off.

Jess walked straight into the sitting room. And there, in Granny's knitting chair, was a Japanese man, exactly as advertised. As Jess entered he leapt to his feet and bowed and smiled. He was quite young, with glossy hair and fabulous velvety brown eyes. He extended his hand.

'Goodnight,' he said. Jess was startled, and shook

hands with him.

'He doesn't really mean goodnight,' warned Granny. 'He said that to me when he first arrived.'

'Noritsugu Nishizawa,' he said, bowing again.

'Goodness knows what that means,' said Granny. 'But keep smiling and don't mention the war.'

'Stop saying things like that in front of him, Granny!' said Jess.

'Oh, don't worry, dear,' said Granny. 'He doesn't understand a word of English. If only your mum would come home. But till she does, I'm afraid we're stuck with him.'

It wasn't exactly the homecoming Jess had been longing for.

7

THOU SHALT NOT WIPE THY NOSE UPON THE CURTAINS, JUST BECAUSE THE TISSUES ARE IN ANOTHER ROOM

'So you've come to see Mum?' asked Jess. 'Er – Madeleine Jordan?'

The Japanese guy handed her a piece of paper.

'That's a letter from your mother,' said Granny.

Jess read it. It said:

Dear Mr Nishizawa,

Thank you very much for expressing an interest in taking lessons in English conversation. I would be pleased to have an initial meeting with you to discuss your requirements on Monday 5th September at 17.30pm.

Yours sincerely,

Madeleine Jordan.

'Ah – you're going to have English lessons with Mum,' Jess said with a polite smile. 'I do remember her saying something about it. I'm sorry she's late. Would you like some tea?'

'It's cold today,' said the Japanese man suddenly and randomly. Was he referring to the weather? Or the tea?

'I offered him some tea when he first arrived,' said Granny, 'and he said *No, please*, so I wasn't sure what to do.'

'So what's the weather like in Japan?' asked Jess, even though she was so tired she could barely keep her eyes open.

'Thank you, that was nice,' he replied.

'I'm sorry Mum's late,' said Jess. 'Oh no! It's ten past six. She's *really* late.'

Suddenly the phone rang out in the kitchen.

''Scuse me,' said Jess, getting up. Just going out to the kitchen felt like a wonderful escape.

'So, have you got any children?' Granny was saying as Jess walked out.

She grabbed the phone. Could it possibly be Fred, replying to her text? Unlikely – he wouldn't use the landline. It was Flora.

'Hi, babe! So how did it go? Have you made it up with Fred?'

63

'Flo! No, I haven't, but I did see his mum, who now hates and despises me – I'll call you back and tell you about it later, OK?' Jess could hear her mum's key in the door and she just had to warn her. 'Gotta go – we've got a random Japanese man on the loose here.'

She rang off and flew to the front door. Her mum was coming in carrying about seven loaded carrier bags of groceries.

'Mum!' whispered Jess. 'A Japanese guy is here! He's in the sitting room! He's been here since 5.30! Where the hell have you been?'

'But I asked him to come at half past seven!' whispered Mum, looking appalled.

'No you didn't, you said 17.30 – he showed me your letter.'

'Oh my God! That wretched twenty-four hour clock! I should have put 19.30 but it always sounds like 9.30!'

One of Mum's carrier bags, which had been slowly giving way, suddenly ripped, and a plastic bag of rice fell to the floor and split.

'I'll sort this out!' said Jess. 'You just go in there and deal with him!'

Mum didn't often take orders from Jess, but this time she just put down the rest of the bags and rushed into the sitting room. Jess fetched the dustpan and brush and began to clear up the mess.

'Mr Nishizawa!' Jess heard her mum say. 'I'm so sorry! I've been completely stupid! I got mixed up between 7.30 and 17.30! I do apologise! I'm completely useless at anything to do with numbers! Do forgive me!'

'Goodnight!' said Mr Nishizawa.

'He means *How do you do*,' said Granny helpfully. 'And he doesn't understand a word of English, dear, so you'd better start at the beginning.'

'Mr Nishizawa!' said Mum. 'Would you like to come upstairs to my study?'

Mum led Mr Nishizawa out of Granny's room. He made a kind of graceful bow towards Jess, who was squatting unattractively in a sea of scattered rice. He also managed to convey, with a sympathetic shrug, his sympathy for the split carrier bag situation. Then he followed Mum upstairs. His shoes were flawless and shiny and a rather wonderful waft of lemony aftershave lingered behind him.

'I suppose we'd better take them up a cup of tea,' said Granny, coming out of her room. 'Madeleine will be gasping for one.'

Jess and Granny unpacked the shopping. There was a packet of rather stylish little biscuits which they'd never had before. Mum had evidently bought these to impress Mr Nishizawa. Jess arranged four on a plate whilst Granny made the tea. Then Jess carried the tray upstairs and knocked on Mum's study door.

'Come in!' called Mum in a rather tight, bright, shiny public voice. As Jess entered she could see that Mum was getting a headache.

'Oh thank you, darling!' cried Mum. 'How kind! Would you like a cup of tea, Mr Nishizawa?'

'Oh thank you, darling,' said Mr Nishizawa, rather startlingly.

'Shall I bring you the paracetamol?' asked Jess.

'Please,' said Mum, looking desperate beneath a thin veneer of relaxation. 'They're in the bathroom cabinet. Do you take milk and sugar, Mr Nishizawa?'

'No please,' he replied. No wonder Mum was getting a headache. Jess fetched the tablets and a glass of water, and left Mum tucking into the first of the smart biscuits, which exploded all over her skirt. It seemed family life in Jess's house was doomed to remain farcical.

Jess went downstairs to find that Granny had laid a little snack for them in the sitting room: tea, orange juice for Jess, and some egg mayonnaise sandwiches.

'I made this egg mayonnaise earlier, dear,' said Granny. 'I know it's your favourite and you'll need something special after your first day at school.'

'Oh Granny, you are a star!' said Jess, kissing her. 'Let's watch *Pulp Fiction*.'

Pulp Fiction was Granny's favourite and normally she would leap at the chance of seeing it for the ninety-ninth time, but now she hesitated.

'I don't know, dear,' she whispered. 'It might disturb your mother.' Granny rolled her eyes towards the ceiling. Mum's study was above, and it wasn't very well insulated. They could hear the murmur of Mum's voice droning away up there, and just occasionally, a few words in a deeper voice from Mr Nishizawa.

'I hope it goes all right,' said Jess. 'She's getting one of her headaches.'

'Well, of course, if she'd put the right time down on his letter, he wouldn't have come till half past seven, and she'd have had time for a bite to eat and a rest,' said Granny. They ate the egg mayonnaise sandwiches in silence, listening to the voices mumbling away upstairs.

'You said you'd had a dreadful day, dear,' said Granny. 'It can't have been as bad as a woman in Bradford. It was on the TV news. There was a gas

67

leak and her house blew up. Nobody was hurt.' Granny looked a bit disappointed at the modest death toll. 'But she'd just had the bedrooms redecorated.'

'She must be gutted,' said Jess. She sighed. There was a moment's silence – even upstairs.

'So tell me about your awful day then, lovey,' said Granny. Jess sighed again. She seemed full of sighs ever since the row with Fred. She wasn't sure whether she could tell Granny the whole story. She didn't want her to think badly of Fred. And though she craved sympathy, she felt so damn tired she could hardly be bothered to embark on the complicated saga of the Christmas Show being replaced, disastrously, by Shakespeare.

Then she noticed something odd. There was still no sound from upstairs. Granny realised it at the same time. They stared up at the ceiling. Not a word.

'Perhaps they're reading something,' said Jess. 'Silently.'

'But he's supposed to be here for English conversation,' said Granny.

They sat and listened some more. No sound. Absolute silence reigned upstairs.

'It's kind of creepy,' said Jess.

'I hope he hasn't murdered her,' said Granny.

Granny was obsessed by homicide and always considered it as a possibility in any situation.

'If he has murdered her,' said Jess, 'he must be just sitting there staring silently at the body.'

'Unless he's escaped through the window,' said Granny. 'But I think we would have heard him landing in the garden.'

They sat and listened for a bit longer. Still there was absolutely no sound from upstairs.

'This is getting really scary,' said Jess. 'What shall we do?'

'Go up and ask if she wants any more tea,' said Granny.

Jess got up, feeling really quite nervous, and tiptoed upstairs. She listened right outside Mum's study door. Silence. Not even the rustle of paper. Terror seized Jess's soul. She tapped lightly on the door, opened it a bit, and looked in.

Amazing sight! Mum was sitting cross-legged on the floor with her eyes closed – and so was Mr Nishizawa.

'Oh, sorry,' said Jess, astonished. 'I just wondered if you wanted some more tea.'

Mum opened her eyes. 'Mr Nishizawa's teaching me to meditate,' she said. 'He saw me taking my headache pills and suggested a moment of contemplation. I feel better already.'

'Oh good,' said Jess. 'Sorry to disturb you.'

As she went out again, she noticed their shoes. They had taken them off and put them by the door. Mr Nishizawa's glistened blackly. They looked extremely smart next to Mum's rank old trainers.

Shortly afterwards Jess fell into a light doze on Granny's sofa. She woke up when Mr Nishizawa left, and helped Mum make a bizarre risotto which included both tuna and bacon. Neither of them was really gifted when it came to cuisine. Jess didn't think they'd have much success if they ever started a dating agency, either. Tuna and bacon! Hardly a match made in heaven.

After supper, Jess lay on the sofa all evening watching TV. Really she was waiting for Fred to send a text message. What on earth was he up to? Where had he been today? Was he suffering agonies, too? She jolly well hoped so. By ten o'clock he still hadn't rung.

'Didn't you have any homework today?' asked Mum suspiciously.

'No – first day back,' explained Jess briskly. Mum seemed to accept it without any trouble, and went off to have a bath.

At half past ten Jess realised she hadn't rung Flora

back. But then, she had nothing to tell her. The situation with Fred was still a deep mystery. And Flora's dad didn't like people ringing after ten because he often had an early night after a long hard day importing bathrooms.

Miserably, Jess dragged herself off to bed. 'Honestly, Rasputin,' she told her bear as her head hit the pillow, 'life sucks at the moment.'

Rasputin was just about to reply when her mobile vibrated. Maybe it was a message from Fred! Her stomach gave a huge, electric leap. Jess grabbed the phone and clicked on the envelope logo. The message was revealed. **THANKS – FRED.**

Jess's heart plummeted a thousand feet and smashed into a frozen lake. She felt her veins freeze with horror. Two words? A mere *two*? When Fred was the king of vocabulary? What sort of message was that? What did it mean? It was a goddam insult.

Jess's blood stopped freezing and instantly started to boil with rage. 'Thanks' was an insult. And what did it mean? Thanks for warning him about his mum knowing he'd bunked off? Or kind of 'Thanks for everything – it's been fun knowing you'? Jess had a dreadful feeling that this was Fred's way of saying goodbye. After that she just couldn't sleep, and it was well past 2am before she fell into a light doze and embarked on a series of bloodcurdling nightmares involving wardrobes with teeth.

8

ORDER NOT WORTHLESS
JUNK FROM EBAY USING THY
MOTHER'S CREDIT CARD

'Jess! It's half past seven! I've called you four times!'
Mum's face suddenly appeared in the middle of a
horrid dream about monkeys. Oh my God! Jess usually got up at seven, which left plenty of time for
breakfast, finding the right shoes, and extensive
restoration work on her eyebrows. Right now she
barely had enough time to throw on her clothes.

Then, with an appalling shock, she suddenly
realised that she hadn't done the extra homework
Miss Thorn had set. She hadn't written an account of
her family. Miss Thorn's laser-like eyes would certainly penetrate as far as her bone marrow at this
news, and leave her a shattered hulk.

There was only one thing to do. Jess leapt out of
bed, pushed past her mum, ran into the bathroom,

and locked the door behind her. She turned on all the taps, filled a glass of water, and then launched into a series of ghastly retching sounds.

'Yeaurk!' she spluttered. 'Heurk! Honk!' She threw glassfuls of water down the loo – kind of pure, delightful puke. Was it convincing?

'Jess!' Her mum knocked on the bathroom door, sounding concerned. 'Are you all right?' Jess suddenly remembered that French sounded like vomiting. She thought of the two boys who'd played a starring role in the French exchange recently: Edouard and Gerard.

'Edouaaard!' she yelled. 'Geraard! Edouaaard!'

'Darling!' cried mum out on the landing. 'Are you being sick?'

'Yeah, I vommed,' croaked Jess. 'Must've been something I ate.'

'Maybe it was that egg mayonnaise,' said Mum thoughtfully. 'Are you all right in there?'

Evidently the French had been very convincing. Jess would recommend it to all her mates. She turned off all the taps, flushed the loo and cleaned her teeth. Then she unlocked the bathroom door and staggered out, trying to look pale and nauseous.

'I'm sorry,' she said. 'I don't think I can go to school this morning. Maybe I'll be OK by lunchtime.'

'Of course, of course,' said Mum, accompanying Jess back into her bedroom, fussing over her and tucking her in. Jess lay tragically on her side. Suddenly her tummy gave a deafening rumble, like distant thunder in the mountains. Secretly, she was absolutely starving.

'Oh dear, your poor tummy is in a state,' said Mum. 'I shouldn't eat anything for a couple of hours.'

'A couple of days, more like,' groaned Jess, fighting off an urge to devour the whole duvet, raw. As soon as Mum had gone off to work, Jess would go downstairs and ransack the fridge. She would tell Granny she felt heaps better. Granny might even be persuaded to make her scrambled eggs. And then she'd do the homework for Miss Thorn.

This plan, like most of Jess's plans, backfired. Granny was delighted to hear Jess was feeling better, but she wasn't in the mood for cooking. She was smartly dressed in old lady's festive clothes, and combing her hair.

'Deirdre is coming in a minute to take me to the club,' said Granny excitedly. 'It's our coffee morning and we usually play a round or two of bridge.'

'You should play poker for money,' said Jess. 'I bet you'd clean up.'

So Jess had to make her own breakfast: cheese

on toast and a mug of hot chocolate. How divine it was, not going to school. Jess looked forward eagerly to her life as an adult, which would involve getting up very late and taking breakfast with her poodle Bonbon on a balcony overlooking the Mediterranean.

Her mum had always insisted that financial independence was terribly important for women, whether they lived alone or with a partner, but Jess thought that if a millionaire turned up and offered her his hand in marriage, together with a house by the sea, that would be just fine. She wasn't fussy – any old millionaire would do.

However, thoughts of love and marriage immediately led back to the awful situation between her and Fred. Since she and Fred had become An Item, she had occasionally fantasised about marrying him and having a couple of stylish and well-behaved children and a whole pack of beautiful dogs, their coats gleaming with conditioner and their breath smelling delightfully of chocolate.

But now this lovely daydream was beginning to wither. Jess wondered if Fred would ever hold her hand again, let alone lead her to the altar. That text message of his last night was so curt, it was like a knife to the heart. 'Thanks – Fred' indeed! A cruel dig disguised as politeness. A diabolical response to her kind warning about his mum being on the warpath.

Jess tried to get her head around the fact that Fred was behaving really horribly to her. The thought made her feel suddenly *really* sick. She must think about something else, quick, or the pretend vomming in French this morning might prove to be a rehearsal for the real thing.

She ran upstairs, went into her mum's study and switched on the PC. She must describe her family so brilliantly that Miss Thorn would be captivated and revise her first bad impression, nay, become her most ardent fan. Jess put on a Nirvana CD – it always seemed to stimulate her brain – and got stuck in.

My parents, strangely, met whilst queuing for a loo. It was at a party in London where they were at college. My mum was immediately attracted by Dad's shoulder-length blond hair and his obsessive interest in a range of skin ailments. He told her he was an art student, which was the thing to be in the olden days. She had already realised he was artistically inclined – his pink velvet jeans gave it away. Although everybody wore pink velvet in those days, so it was kind of a fashion cliché.

At first she didn't suspect that he was gay. It was only years later when he moved to St Ives and set up house with a surfer called Phil that her suspicions were aroused. And when she found them dancing The Time Warp with Phil dressed as a frog, she had to accept that hers was not a conventional marriage.

Mum has adjusted quite well to being tragically abandoned by a gay hypochondriac. She has seized the opportunity to mope about being ill herself, although she does it with much less panache than Dad. With Mum it's just boring, unglamorous headaches. But Dad frequently sends me text messages describing his latest symptoms, always of some rare and stylish fatal disease. He has a pet seagull called Horace, which he probably prefers to having custody of me.

Mum's mum, known with stunning originality as Granny, lives with us. Grandpa died recently and Granny kept his ashes on the coffee table for months so he could watch the football. Grandpa used to have a party trick which he would perform in pubs: biting the head off a live rat. He would never do it for me, though. It was an 18-and-over kind of thing.

Granny is also quite bloodthirsty. She is completely addicted to homicide – as an onlooker, I mean, not a participant (yet). Her favourite movie is Pulp Fiction *which she finds more sophisticated than* Robocop *– though no* *less gruesome. When young, Granny was wooed by a strange nerd-like man called Gordon Cranston. He proposed marriage and she refused him, because she did not like the way feathers grew out of his arse. Tragically, he was shot by a farmer whilst grazing harmlessly on a field of young wheat.*

Jess read through her homework. It was OK, except possibly that stupid bit at the end about Gordon Cranston. That was the only bit she had made up. It had been absolute torture, having to stick to the truth, but up till then she had managed it. Jess deleted the Gordon Cranston bit and printed it out.

Delightful though it would have been to spend the whole day at home, she was desperate to get back to school and see Fred. They absolutely had to sort things out if she was ever to have a decent night's sleep again.

First she whizzed off a text message to Mum. AM BETTER AND GOING IN FOR AFTERNOON SCHOOL. LOVE, JESS. She would get a few Brownie points for her plucky recovery. She also left an affectionate note for Granny. And then she set off.

It was much nicer walking to school at lunchtime. It was sunny and warm, and instead of people rushing to work, there were mums out with little pre-school kids and old people having fun exercising their dogs. Jess began to feel a bit more hopeful.

Suddenly she had a brilliant, brilliant idea of how to improve her rather gloomy situation. During the summer she and Fred had spent long days in the park writing comedy sketches, preparing for the Christmas Show. They knew Mr Fothergill would want them to do at least one sketch, maybe even two. Now, with the show cancelled and Mr Fothergill in hospital, that delightful prospect seemed to have disappeared.

But it didn't have to! Once she'd made things up with Fred, they could plan a whole show of sketches – maybe with a couple of songs by Flora's band, Poisonous Trash. They could put the show on anyway, *as well as* Miss Thorn's production of *Twelfth Night*! Jess was sure she could get permission to use the school hall. Mrs Tomkins the head teacher always liked initiative. And what could be more enterprising than organising a whole comedy show?

Maybe they could even get an agent to come and see it! Maybe the agent would manage to get a TV company interested! Maybe Jess and Fred would become a famous comedy duo and take the world by storm!

Jess arrived at school fizzing and buzzing with the

prospect of a brilliant career, and went straight to the cafeteria, where she expected to find Flora and, with any luck, Fred. She hadn't wanted to see him in a public place but she didn't really have a choice – in fact it might be a bit easier at first for them to meet with lots of other people about.

However, there was nobody much in the cafeteria except Ben Jones. He was talking to another footballing guy called Marcus Dawson, but he looked up when Jess came in and gave her a big smile and an inviting wave. At least somebody was pleased to see her.

'Hi!' said Jess, including Marcus in her greeting as he was rather a sweet person though his nose resembled a turnip and he smelt slightly of mice. 'Have you seen Flora or – er – Fred?'

'Ah, oh yeah, they've both gone to audition for *Twelfth Night*,' said Ben. 'Are you going too? Or you could go tomorrow, right? Wanna cheeseburger or are you on salad today?'

Jess could not speak for a moment. OK, she knew that Flora was going to audition for *Twelfth Night*, but the fact that Fred was also up for a part in it was the worst news ever. If Fred turned out to be starring in *Twelfth Night*, no way was he going to have time for the comedy show with her. In fact, Jess began to wonder if he was ever going to have time for her again.

'Yeah,' said Jess rather limply. 'What the hell. Give me a cheeseburger, straight into the vein.'

9

BITE NOT THY NAILS NEITHER GROW LONG ONES LIKE TALONS

There was a class registration at the start of afternoon school. Jess knew Fred would be there. It would be the first time they had been together since that ludicrous scene in the park. Jess was desperate, desperate to get back together with him. Life had been agony since their row. But all the same she dreaded seeming needy.

She got to the classroom early, before everybody else. When Fred arrived, she wouldn't want to be sitting alone kind of staring hopefully at the door, so she decided to grab the first person who entered and have a vivacious and attractive conversation with them. There were windows overlooking a path through the school garden, and people who were heading for Jess's classroom often walked down this path, so you could see them coming.

Jess saw a girl called Beatrice Poole, affectionately known as Poo-face. Beatrice waved. Jess was glad it was going to be Beatrice, as she was extremely giggly and would be easy to amuse. The door opened.

'Hi, Poo-face!' yelled Jess. But, disaster! It was Miss Thorn. There was another way to get to the classroom, unfortunately: down the corridor. People who chose this route arrived unexpectedly. Miss Thorn closed the door behind her and glared at Jess.

'I'm sorry,' said Jess, blushing. 'I thought you were somebody else.'

'Why were you absent this morning?' asked Miss Thorn.

'I was sick,' said Jess.

'Do you have a letter from your mother or father?'

'Er – no,' said Jess. 'My mum works in the library, so she had to go off early. I think she was expecting me to be ill all day. I can bring a note tomorrow.'

'Yes, please do,' said Miss Thorn. 'And what about your homework?'

Jess handed it over. Somehow it had got a bit crumpled in the cafeteria, and there were a couple of ketchup splashes on it. Miss Thorn held it fastidiously and her savage eyes devoured the page. Again, she showed no reaction. Her face was a mask. Jess almost wished she'd left in the bit about Granny's fictional suitor who had the feathers growing out of his arse.

Miss Thorn finished reading and looked up. For a moment they locked eyes. Jess felt uncomfortable.

'You'll never make a journalist,' said Miss Thorn brusquely.

'I don't want to be a journalist,' said Jess, feeling quite insulted. 'I'm going to be a stand-up comedian.'

Miss Thorn sighed and shook her head as though dealing with someone of very limited intelligence.

'It's a rough old trade,' she said. 'I wouldn't want any daughter of mine to go into it.'

Jess had a brief and horrible hallucination in which she was Miss Thorn's daughter. She arrived home every evening to dine in silence on a thistle omelette off a stainless steel plate. She then did her homework for five hours, and afterwards endured a light thrashing with a hairbrush before being locked in an unheated bedroom. She slept on a hard mattress on a wrought-iron bed. There was a CCTV camera in the bathroom, and even her teddy bear was bald and hostile.

The classroom door opened and a gang of kids came in: Beatrice, but also Gina and Tom and Caz and Jules. They looked surprised to see Miss Thorn, and their conversation sort of died.

'Sit down,' said Miss Thorn. They all scattered. Jess started to make her escape towards the back of the room.

'I haven't finished with you, Jess Jordan,' said Miss Thorn. 'I'll accept this piece of work as a goodwill gesture, despite its facetious tone. But I will not accept paper which is covered with filth.'

'Bog roll?' said Tom softly. Beatrice giggled. Miss Thorn ignored them. She was still glaring at Jess.

'Copy it out neatly on to a clean piece of paper,' she said, holding out the original. Jess took it out of her hand. She was so tempted to snatch it, but she knew if she did she would be in deep, deep trouble. She went to the back of the room and sat next to Caz.

The door opened and another group walked in. Flora was there, and she grinned at Jess and came right over. Still no Fred. A few stragglers entered. Still no Fred. Jess's heart started to pound madly.

'Right,' said Miss Thorn, 'in a minute, there's going to be a –'

The door swung open and Fred strolled in. Jess's

whole body kind of exploded. He looked a hundred times nicer than she remembered. He grinned cheerily at Miss Thorn, then turned and, for a moment, their eyes met, and then,

BRRRRRRRRRRRRRRRRRRRRRING! BRRRRRRRRRRRRRRRRING!

The most deafening bell started to ring.

'It's the fire alarm!' said Gina.

'It's a Fred alarm!' said Tom.

'OK!' shouted Miss Thorn. 'Walk in an orderly fashion and assemble on the field!'

'Of course it is important, if one is being burnt to death, to perish in an orderly fashion,' said Jess as they all marched out. Flora grinned, and once they were out in the corridor she grabbed Jess's arm.

'I had the most fantastic time at the auditions, Jess,' she yelled (the bell made confidences rather difficult). 'I read a scene with this new guy who's just come into the Upper Sixth. God, he was ubergorgeous! His name's Jack Stevens and he's got five-star eyelashes!'

Jess was hardly listening. She was mesmerised by the sight, twenty yards ahead, of Fred's back as he marched off down the corridor talking to Buster Beresford, without even turning round to pull a satirical face at her. Fred was blanking her! He was just kind of strolling along talking to Buster of all people! Buster who frequently insulted Fred and was basically a no-brain. Jess could hardly believe her eyes.

'God, babe, he's so gorgeous.' Flora was jabbering away in her ear about the hunky new guy at the auditions but Jess could not concentrate on anything. The certainty that Fred hated her was squeezing the breath out of her, rather like a size 10 Lycra top.

Out in the schoolyard they all lined up and the teachers took registration, but Fred still avoided her. Then the normal bell rang for afternoon lessons. Jess was desperate to escape, to get out of Fred's company. Luckily it was food technology this afternoon, not one of Fred's options. They had often discussed how they would spend their future lives on the sofa and never cook, just ring for a pizza to be delivered. But now it seemed they would never even speak again, let alone share a DVDs 'n' Junk Food To Go lifestyle.

Flora didn't do food technology either – she was obviously going to be rich enough to hire a chef.

'OK – see you at 3.30 by the gates?' whispered Flora. 'We might even see Jack Stevens. I can't wait for you to meet him!'

Jess nodded in an automatic kind of way, but she felt blind and deaf. Fred was walking off with a gang of lads, and they burst into a huge explosion of laughter. Maybe they were laughing at her! She had to get out of here!

Jess ran through the maze of corridors to the food technology department. Never had Mrs Kendall's room been such a sanctuary. Although food technology was one of Jess's favourite subjects, of course. Today there was a delightful smell of coconut cake in the air. But Jess couldn't have managed even a mouthful. She felt so sick with anxiety, there was just a chance she might manage to lose a few pounds before finally dying of a broken heart round about 4.30 on Friday afternoon.

'Today we're going to look at the calorific value of different sorts of fats,' said Mrs Kendall, leaning on the teacher's desk. The veins in her wrists bulged horribly. Jess closed her eyes for an instant and tried to clear her mind of all thoughts of Fred, and replace them with polyunsaturated margarine. But instead she endured a nightmarish vision of Fred coated in butter, wrestling with Ben Jones.

Love, Sex and Stuff was so distracting. Not for the first time, Jess wished there were no such things as male persons in the world, and women could reproduce just by cloning themselves in a jamjar on the bathroom shelf. Although the thought of a small version of herself, complete with flab, clumsiness and stupidity, was kind of hard to bear.

At the end of school Jess found Flora by the gates. She looked disappointed and grabbed Jess by the arm.

'You missed him!' she hissed. 'He gave me this amazing smile, but that tall girl with a red ponytail was monopolising him!'

Jess agreed, without really concentrating, that this was indeed appalling, and they set off home. Jess had so often walked home with Fred that every paving stone seemed to miss him.

'Let's go to the Dolphin and get ourselves some nachos,' said Flora. Jess suddenly felt hungry. She was tired of being heartbroken. Why should she risk malnutrition just because Fred was behaving like a dingbat?

'Yeah,' she agreed heartily. 'Or maybe a cheese-burger and fries.'

In fine weather there were tables out on the pavement, but you had to go in and queue for your food first.

'Hey! There's a free table!' said Flora. 'You sit there and bag it and I'll go in and get the grub. Nachos and Coke be OK?'

'Diet Coke – no, juice! Juice!' said Jess. She was determined to start a new life right here and now.

She would torment Fred by becoming fabulous. She would be slim, elegant, intellectually brilliant and fabulously wealthy. OK, so it would take a few days, but she was damned if she was going to dwindle away into a small sickly lovesick pool of lovesick. Hell, who needed boys? There would always be dogs – so loyal, so true.

She was just trying to decide whether a Golden Retriever or a Red Setter would suit her elegant new hair colour (she was planning to go a lustrous chestnut by the weekend) when the door to the Dolphin Café opened and three boys clattered out laughing. Buster, Tom, and – disastrously – Fred.

He couldn't really pretend he hadn't seen her, because her table was right there by the door. So he sort of paused for a minute.

'Miss Jordan!' he said, in a kind of haughty public voice. 'Are you still alive? I thought you must have been barbecued in that rather convenient fire earlier today.' Buster and Tom laughed, the morons.

'So sorry to disappoint you,' replied Jess, as a great surge of adrenalin rushed up her throat and fizzed all over her face like fireworks. 'I thought you were the one who'd perished in the blaze actually – I was sure I got a whiff of roast pork.' Buster and Tom laughed again, even louder. This comforted Jess slightly.

'Come on, Parsons,' said Buster.

'We have an appointment at the video hire place,' said Fred with a shrug. 'With a few thousand Orcs, I believe.'

'I do so understand,' said Jess. 'In fact, you could all become Orcs yourselves without any need for cosmetic surgery.'

'We'll leave the cosmetic surgery to you, Miss Jordan,' said Fred. 'Except I suppose your only problem would be, where to begin?'

The boys laughed and went off. Jess just went on grinning in what she hoped was a devastatingly sarcastic way, although she was barely able to stop the tears from bursting from her eyes.

She and Fred had always swapped scathing insults, but not like this, not in public, not with the horrible feeling that they were really meant to hurt. Why was he being so cruel?

'I got you Passion Fruit and Orange, is that OK?' said Flora, arriving with the tray.

Jess wasn't sure she could face food or drink after all, least of all Passion Fruit. It was passion which had got her into this mess in the first place.

'Mmmm! Don't these nachos smell wonderful!' purred Flora, unfolding her paper napkin and placing it on her happy little lap. Jess began to feel she wasn't living in the same world. She was secretly in one of the blackest pits of hell, and it was going to take heroism of the highest order to claw her way back to the daylight.

10

BURP NOT LOUDLY IN THE STREET: IT IS NOT MAIDENLY

Flora was so happy, kind of fizzing with excitement about Jack and *Twelfth Night* and everything, that Jess felt it was completely the wrong moment to break the devastating news that her life was over. She couldn't possibly ruin Flora's day. Could she?

'Look, sorry to sound like a tragedy queen,' she burst out after the second nacho, 'but my life is over, as it were.'

'What?' said Flora, her eyes wide in amazement. Jess briefly ran through the whole Fred saga, culminating in his recent hideous insults.

'But you guys always talk to each other like that,' said Flora. 'It's so cool. He's mad about you, it's obvious. This is just a glitch, babe.'

'Really?' asked Jess, feeling rather like a sad dog

who has just been whipped and meets a kind young maiden who strokes his ears instead. 'Do you think so?'

'Yeah, look, this can be sorted, easy,' said Flora, licking guacamole off her perfect lips. 'Soon as you get home, just call him. Say something like, *Come on, for God's sake Fred, let's stop this insane messing about and get back to normal.* Or something. You're much more eloquent than I am – you'll think of something better. It'll all be sorted in a few seconds, believe me.'

Jess felt encouraged. 'Thanks, you heavenly creature,' she said, reaching out and squeezing Flora's hand. 'May you live for ever in a paradise of palm trees, fast cars and samba music.'

'Sounds like Hollywood,' said Flora. 'That's Plan B if New York won't have me.'

'Whole continents will fight over you,' Jess assured her. 'Don't confine yourself to mere cities. Think big.'

They went back to talking about the new boy and whether or not the girl with the red ponytail could be humanely despatched before she managed to fascinate him.

Jess arrived home feeling much more positive. She would ignore all this foolishness of recent days. She would just ring Fred and bring him to heel. It would be the work of a moment. She wouldn't send a text. That was cowardly. He was probably even now longing for his phone to ring. OK, it was slightly annoying that she had to be the one to make the move, but males were really clueless when it came to relationships.

Hastily Jess looked around the house to see how the land lay. Mum was in the garden with Mr Nishizawa.

'What, is he back again?' said Jess to Granny as they peeped out of the kitchen window.

'He's having a lesson every evening, apparently – a crash course,' said Granny, who was making a cup of tea. 'He's not here for long. He's got to go back to Japan at the end of the month.'

Jess was glad to hear it. She didn't have anything against Mr Nishizawa personally. Indeed he was about as cool as they came. But she just hated the idea of Mum always being busy with strangers in the evenings, when her main duty should have lain in selfless slavery to her immediate family. However, right now it was convenient to have Mum out of earshot. Jess was nerving herself up for the phone call to Fred.

Granny toddled off to watch the news. ('There's been a terrible fire in Australia, dear – but they've managed to save some of the koalas.') The kitchen phone was now divinely free and private. It was the perfect moment. Jess dialled Fred's home number and waited with a thudding heart. Fred's mum answered.

'Hi! This is Jess. Could I speak to Fred, please?'

'Oh, sorry, Jess,' said Fred's mum. 'But he's not home yet. Apparently he's gone over to – what's his name? – Buster's. They're doing a project on *The Lord of the Rings*, or so he said.'

'Doing a project, yeah,' said Jess ironically, trying to ignore the sinking of her heart. 'Pigging out in front of mythical violence for the hundredth time, more like.'

'You're so right,' said Fred's mum. 'Anyway, you can try his mobile. He might have it switched on.'

'Yeah, OK,' said Jess. 'Thanks. See you soon.'

'I hope so,' said Fred's mum, with just the faintest hint of regret. 'We haven't seen you for a day or two, have we? Well, come round any time. You know you'll always be welcome.' Fred's mum had certainly noticed something. Jess rang off trying to sound as cheery as possible, even though her heart had plummeted back towards the boiling centre of the earth.

She couldn't possibly phone Fred on his mobile while he was watching *The Lord of the Rings* with Tom and Buster eavesdropping on his every word. She would just have to wait.

Jess was suddenly desperately lonesome. She went to Granny's room, eager to share even the TV news with her. She was prepared to sit through a whole succession of natural disasters, terrorist outrages and tragic famines if only she could hold Granny's hand.

But Granny was asleep. How damned tactless! Jess sighed with exasperation, quite loudly, hoping that Granny might hear and awake, open her cute little old arms and say, 'Give me a cuddle, darling! I feel so depressed after that weather forecast.'

But no. Granny dozed on, her lips rippling slightly with each breath. 'No, John!' she said suddenly, and smiled in her sleep. My God! Granny was dreaming about Grandpa! Possibly raunchily! Possibly, in her dreams, they were both twenty again …

Jess tiptoed hastily out. She didn't want to overhear any elderly naughtiness. If only Mum was available. But she was still sitting out in the garden with Mr Nishizawa. There was a kind of picnic table with a couple of benches down the far end of the garden, and they were down there having their English Conversation, even though the sun had already sunk well below the neighbour's hawthorn hedge.

I know, thought Jess, *I'll offer them some tea. Then I*

might at least find out when he's going. She put on a sweet and innocent smile. It wasn't really her sort of thing, but somehow she felt on her best behaviour with Mr Nishizawa around.

'Hi, Mum! Mr Nishizawa!' said Jess. They looked up, and Mr Nishizawa leapt to his feet, which was quite hard to do when you're sitting at a picnic table with integral benches. He bowed, and his brown eyes sparkled. God, was he the business!

'Good evening!' he said, then, laughing, he turned to Mum. 'Not Goodnight!' he added. They both laughed, for what seemed like a rather insanely long time.

'Yes,' said Jess, wanting to move the conversation on. '*Good evening*, very good, terrific. Sorry to disturb you, Mum, but I wondered if you would like some tea?'

'Oh, no thanks, love,' said Mum. 'And by the way, we're going out tonight. Nori is taking me to a concert. A Japanese pianist is playing and Nori knows him slightly. We'll go round afterwards and probably have a drink with him or something, so I might be back a bit late. Don't wait up.'

'Wow, fantastic!' said Jess, trying not to betray her deep disappointment and disgust at this news. 'Have fun. Oh, by the way, Mum – could you write me a note for tomorrow, please? About missing school this morning because of my tummy upset?'

'Yes, sure, of course, darling,' said Mum, turning back to Mr Nishizawa. Or, as he was apparently now known, 'Nori'. 'Shall we break for lunch?'

Lunch? thought Jess. *What the hell is she talking about?*

'Shall we break for lunch?' repeated Mr Nishizawa hesitantly. Oh, it wasn't a conversation. It was a 'Conversation'. Things were so confusing these days.

Jess went back indoors and comforted herself with loud music. At a certain stage she was aware of Mum and Mr Nishizawa leaving for their night out. It seemed Mum was the one having all the fun these days.

After listening to her most depressing CDs for two hours, Jess felt life was so futile she might as well do her homework for once. After wrestling for ten minutes with such unpleasant concepts as Saturated Fats, Polyunsaturated Fats and – worst of all, apparently – Hydrogenated Fats, she began to feel extremely fat even by her standards. She spent an hour trying on Mum's old hippy clothing whilst Granny, refreshed by her nap, gossiped away on the phone to her new friend Iris.

Jess was only too aware that with Granny on the

phone, Fred couldn't ring, and she checked her mobile every twenty minutes to see if he'd texted her. Eventually she just gave up on everything and lay in the bath, shaving her legs again and again until they shone like boiled eggs.

But although at the time Jess felt she was enduring one of the most miserable evenings of her life, compared to what was going to happen tomorrow, it was the calm before the storm.

11

THRUST NOT HALF-EATEN SANDWICHES UNDER THY BED – THE MICE WILL SOON TURN UP

Jess arrived at school next day determined to treat Fred with sunny indifference – if indeed she ever found herself in his company. But as she and Flora were on their way to registration, she suddenly realised that her mum had forgotten to write the letter explaining her absence.

'Oh my God!' she gasped. 'I'll have to forge it! Quick! Let's do it in the loos!' They dived into the girls' toilets.

'But we'll be late!' said Flora, looking pale and panicky.

'It won't take me a min!' said Jess, sitting on the floor by the washbasins and grabbing her rough book and a pen. She ripped a page out of the rough book and put her address at the top of the page, in her mum's rather scatty italic handwriting.

'What about an envelope?' asked Flora, hanging about nervously by the door. The bell had already gone for registration and Flora hated being even half a minute late.

'Never mind – I'll tell her my mum's so disorganised we've run out of envelopes,' said Jess. 'It isn't even a lie. I hate Thorn so much I'm tempted to invent some kind of totally obscene ailment. Like, *Sorry Jess was absent from school yesterday morning but her arse fell off.*'

Flora cracked up. Jess felt encouraged. She always felt kind of safe if she was making people laugh.

'Or like, you know, *Her intestinal wind was so bad it blew the windows out and we had to call the fire brigade.*'

Flora laughed again, even more loudly, although Jess knew that the second joke wasn't quite so funny as the first. But Flora was getting a bit hysterical, because she was so nervous about being late. In this state she would laugh at anything.

'Or, *I apologise for my daughter Jess's lateness yesterday but she gave birth at 6am to a handsome turbot.*'

Flora dissolved into peals of laughter, leaning against the doorpost and gasping. Jess finished off her note – which incidentally was really just a line or two about the tummy upset.

'Luckily I've been forging my mum's signature for years,' she said. 'I'm just waiting for my opportunity to nick her credit card!' She looked up with a grin, and then her blood ran cold. Miss Thorn was standing behind Flora with her arms folded, watching them with complete contempt, and Jess had the feeling she'd been there for ages. And Flora hadn't even noticed!

'Miss Thorn!' said Jess, trying to sound as if she was in control of the situation and delighted to see her favourite teacher. Flora whirled round and kind of froze solid. 'I'm sorry we're late. I just – felt a bit ... a bit sick.' Jess stuffed the letter into her bag and scrambled to her feet. Miss Thorn walked slowly forward and held out her hand.

'I believe that letter is for me?' she said, in a voice as sweet as sulphuric acid.

Jess got it out and dumbly handed it over. There was absolutely no point in trying to say anything perky and attractive. She had to admit she was so NOT in control of the situation.

Miss Thorn perused the letter, then looked up. Lightning flashed from her eyes. Thunder rolled around the craggy heights of her hostility. Jess did notice a tiny speck of dandruff on Miss Thorn's immaculate shoulder. But it wasn't much comfort.

'Flora, you can go and wait for me in the classroom,' she said. Flora flinched and sort of lurched off, looking both guilty and relieved. 'Now, I've had about enough hassle from you,' said Miss Thorn. Her use of the word 'hassle' wasn't lovable – somehow it made her seem even more like a gangster. And her failure to use Jess's name was especially chilling.

'Late on Day One, writing rubbish instead of your essay, absent on Day Two without any note, and now I find you forging one.' Her cold steely eyes slid over Jess with contempt. 'You can go and explain yourself to Mr Powell,' she said, tearing up Jess's letter with a contemptuous flourish and handing the pieces back to Jess.

Jess's legs went cold and started to shake. She turned and walked off towards the admin centre where the Heads of Year had their various offices. She was so terrified, the slightest thing could set off a horrendous bout of projectile vomiting. She was sure if Mr Powell shouted at her, she might just vom straight in his face.

Mr Powell was immensely tall and had big chubby cheeks and curly fair hair. However, despite his curls and dimples he was not heavenly or jolly. He strode about with a frown, looking rather like an angel who has had a row with God. And when he lost his temper he went bright red and shouted so loud you could hear him all over the school. And everybody who heard him reacted with synchronised cringing.

Jess arrived at his door and knocked very timidly. There was no reply. Jess waited. She listened. She couldn't hear anybody moving inside. She looked up and down the corridor. There was nobody about. She felt, in all conscience, she ought to knock once more, properly: loudly. She knocked again, but somehow it turned out even softer, like a fairy wearing velvet gloves knocking on the door of a dormouse who might possibly be asleep. Jess waited. There was no reply.

Suddenly, the bell rang for the start of lessons. Jess bounded swiftly away. There was always the chance that Mr Powell had been meditating, or sucking a throat sweet or something, and she didn't want him to come barging out and find her loitering. But she would have to go and see him later. At lunchtime. Perhaps. In case Miss Thorn checked up on her.

Jess headed for the languages department where she must now endure French. Turning a corner slightly too fast, she bumped straight into Miss Thorn. Jess blushed.

'What did he say?' demanded Miss Thorn.

'He said he was very disappointed in me,' said Jess, so flustered that the disastrous lies came spilling out of her mouth almost before she could think. Wait, that didn't sound much like Mr Powell. Mr Powell had never been *disappointed* in his life. Only incandescent with rage. 'He said it was a diabolical start to the term and if I was sent to him again he'd make me regret I'd ever been born,' added Jess, trying to make it sound more Mr Powellish.

Miss Thorn nodded approvingly. 'As far as I'm concerned, you're on a warning,' she said. 'Just one more problem, and you'll be back in his office straight away.'

Jess shivered with fear. 'Yes, of course,' she said. 'I'm sorry I've been so disorganised so far, but we've got problems at home. My dog is dying of a horrible disease.'

Miss Thorn's eyes flared slightly. 'I'm sorry to hear that, of course,' she said, 'but we all have problems in our home lives which are nothing to do with school. It's your job to carry out your educational duties without getting distracted or making excuses. I want a letter from your mother or father tomorrow without fail.'

And she snapped her lips shut as if they were a high-class laptop, turned on her heel and clicked off.

There was only one thing Jess could do now: descend into torment. It would only be a matter of time before Miss Thorn met Mr Powell. Maybe they would enjoy a cup of coffee together at mid-morning break.

And Miss Thorn would say, 'Thanks so much, Clarence' (or whatever his name was), 'for terrifying the living daylights out of that monstrous brat Jess Jordan.'

Then Mr Powell would start that dreadful pre-yelling warm-up. He would frown, and once he'd realised what a terrible crime Jess had committed, pretending to have seen him whilst being too cowardly to knock properly, well, steam would start to rise from his ears, and he'd come thundering out of the staffroom. He'd hunt her down, and his terrible shouting would turn her entire skeleton to cottage cheese. In public.

12

READ NOT IN THE BATH LEST YE DROP THE BOOK AND RUIN IT

Jess almost enjoyed the French lesson. At least it was safer than the dangerous free-range experience out in the corridors. Out there Miss Thorn could pounce out of a shadowy corner and show her terrible yellow fangs. Or one might hear the distant howling of Mr Powell as he sniffed around the inert body of one of his victims.

At break Flora had to go to the music department, but it was quite near Mr Powell's room, so Jess needed to be very much elsewhere. She said she felt like some fresh air and went out and sat in the furthest corner of the school field. Immediately she became aware that it had rained in the night, and she had sat down on a swamp. She got up in a kneeling position to examine the back of her skirt, and then realised she was also kneeling in mud.

Oh my God, thought Jess in horror, examining the back of her skirt. It was covered with a huge smear of mud. It made her look like a toddler who has had what is diplomatically called 'an accident'. What could she do? There was only one thing for it: an enormous panic attack. She was halfway through her first silent scream when she heard someone call her name. She looked up. It was Ben Jones!

Hastily Jess sat down again. She didn't want Ben to think she had pooed in her pants. As she sat down, though, her bum kind of skidded on the muddy patch, her skirt slid up, and she felt, with awful certainty, that her underpants had also acquired a ghastly brown smear. She pulled down her skirt, covered her muddy knees with her bag, and tried to switch on a sophisticated and elegant smile.

'What's the matter?' he asked, squatting down beside her. *Squatting* sounds kind of undignified, but Ben managed to do it with style. He was more kind of *hunkering down on his haunches* like some sort of chic cowboy by a camp fire.

'What's the *matter*?' sighed Jess. 'Where do I begin?'

She couldn't bear Ben to know about her mud

110

crisis. She didn't really want to mention her problems with Fred. And she didn't even want to *think* about the looming trouble with Miss Thorn and Mr Powell.

'Oh, you know,' she said, 'I'm a bit fed up because we're not having the Show this year. The Christmas Revue thing we usually have. I hate Thorn. She's a total beast.'

'You said you and Fred had written loads of – er, sketches, yeah?' said Ben.

'Yeah,' Jess sighed again – more deeply this time, remembering her wonderful summer with Fred. 'Well, maybe a few.'

'Well, why don't you do a show anyway?' said Ben. 'You could put it on in the lunch break or something. You know – the week before Christmas. There's always loads of extra stuff going on then.'

'I did have that idea myself,' said Jess. 'But it would be a nightmare to organise it all on my own.'

'I'll help,' said Ben. 'I'd do, well, anything. Although I am a dumbo, so I know it wouldn't be much.'

Suddenly, far away in the school, the bell rang for the end of break. Ben got to his feet with an agile leap and held out his hand to pull Jess up.

'There's a problem,' said Jess, staying put. 'Just

before you arrived, I realised I'd sat down on some kind of primeval swamp. My lower clothing is covered with what looks disastrously like cack. Don't laugh.'

She grabbed Ben's hand, he hauled her up, and they both inspected the back of Jess's skirt. Ben didn't laugh at all. He looked concerned and sympathetic.

'You can borrow my football shorts,' said Ben. 'I brought a clean pair today. They're in my locker.'

Jess wasn't sure whether to be touched or appalled. Shorts were so *not* her thing. It was something to do with the shape of her thighs. In shorts, she looked like a cello on holiday. But here was nice, kind Ben Jones offering his very own! A year ago she would have fainted with delight. And candidly, what choice did she have?

'OK, thanks,' she said, staring in horror at the mud slick on her arse. 'But how am I going to get to your locker without everybody seeing?'

Ben took off his jacket, an ultra-cool basketball-style garment in navy blue with the words NEW YORK across the back. He held it out to her.

'Here – tie it round your waist,' he said. 'It'll hide the – erm – mud.'

'But your jacket will get covered with mud!' said Jess.

'It's washable,' grinned Ben. 'And I was too hot anyway.'

'You are my ultimate Guardian Angel!' said Jess, tying the jacket round her waist. Thank God the arms were quite long. The muddy patch at the back was totally covered, and the arms kind of swung about in front, veiling the full horror of her muddy knees.

'Oh God, I'm going to be late – again!' said Jess, looking at her watch. With a sickening lurch she realised it was English next lesson. Miss Thorn would certainly eat her alive. 'I'm in big trouble!' wailed Jess, and set off in what she suspected was a strange duck-like waddling run. Ben jogged at her side with ease. It must be so wonderful to be physically fit.

By the time they reached the corridors there was hardly anybody about. This was later than Jess had ever been. They raced to Ben's locker, and he got out the sacred shorts. Jess accepted them with a mixture of gratitude and foreboding. Would they even fit? Ben's bum was so tiny. Not that she had ever studied it. Well, not for months, anyway.

'Go and try them on in the girls' loos,' said Ben. 'I'll go to physics now, OK? Don't want to hang around the girls' loos – might get a, um – reputation. Some kind of perv. We could go out at lunchtime if you like – there's a launderette next to the Dolphin.' And with a shy smile, he was gone.

Jess ran to the girls' loos, locked herself in a cubicle and ripped off her skirt. She also took off her knickers and examined the damage. A vast smear of mud, still wet and oozy, was plastered right across the back of both skirt and knickers. She couldn't wear Ben's shorts on top of that. It would ruin the shorts, and the horrible muck might even drip down her legs … urghhh!

There was no choice: she had to cram herself into Ben's shorts. Thank God they were not too small. And thank God there wasn't a full-length mirror in the girls' loos. Jess just knew she looked like some overweight bumpkin out of a children's nursery rhyme. She bundled up her skirt and knickers and zipped them into a secret inner pocket of her schoolbag. And then she swiftly washed the mud from her knees, and ventured out into the corridors.

For an instant she was tempted to go straight home. That would solve everything. She could wash her dirty clothes there; maybe even find a clean skirt and rush back to school. But it was strictly forbidden to bunk off school without permission. They'd been extra-vigilant about it ever since a girl called Alice had sneaked off to meet a boy she had got to know on the internet, and he had turned out to be a paedophile in his fifties. Luckily Alice had escaped with a single bound (she was high-jump champion) but it had made all the grown-ups very edgy.

Only one course of action was open to Jess. She had to go to English. Already about fifteen minutes late, Jess approached the classroom with intense dread. She opened the door a crack, and tried to creep in very slowly, unobserved. But the door was right at the front, next to Miss Thorn, who was reading a war poem in a tragic voice.

'*My soul looked down from a vague height, with Death ...*'

Jess wanted desperately to turn round and go out again, but she was already halfway into the room. As the class saw her in Ben's shorts, they just could not help themselves: there was an explosion of laughing. There was only one person in the room who wasn't laughing: Fred. He looked embarrassed and weird.

Miss Thorn turned from her book. It seemed to Jess that she wheeled to face her almost in slow motion. With a terrible long cruel glare Miss Thorn took in the vision of Jess standing there in her ridiculous shorts, with her silly fat knees, like some kind of terrible clown. The gales of laughter went on and on, blowing away the serious, tragic atmosphere of the war poetry. Miss Thorn's face turned to granite and Jess knew her life was over.

13

WATCH NOT MTV
MORE THAN AN HOUR
A DAY LEST THY BRAIN
TURN TO CHEESE

Miss Thorn turned her cold eyes to the class, and somehow the laughter faded. Jess was usually pleased when people laughed at her, but not this time. She tried to stand there looking dignified, but it was hopeless.

'I'm not wasting any more time on you,' said Miss Thorn. 'No doubt Mr Powell will be surprised to see you again so soon. Off you go – now.'

Jess was only too glad to leave the room. She closed the door behind her and stood in the corridor for a few seconds, fighting off a terrible desire to burst into tears.

Fred had looked so shocked and appalled. He was embarrassed ever to have been a slight acquaintance of hers, never mind An Item. Maybe what he'd said in the park hadn't been a joke after all. 'If everybody knows we're together I shall lose whatever street cred I ever had.' Maybe he really *had* been scared of looking like 'a doting nerd'. And now that she'd made a complete spectacle of herself, he'd never speak to her again.

She had been kind of hoping that if she could only get him on his own for a moment, she'd be able to say a few magic words, and everything would be back to normal. But Fred had a habit of going into his shell and sulking if misunderstandings arose. He hated and feared rows. Even before they'd got together he'd blanked her for weeks just because he thought she was with Ben Jones.

What on earth could she do now? How does a girl retrieve her dignity when it lies in a million pieces at her feet? How does a girl retrieve her dignity whilst wearing football shorts which are a bit too tight and reveal her fat knees and massive bum? How could she possibly go to see Mr Powell without proper protective clothing? If he shouted at her in her present outfit, she feared her knees would buckle with nakedness and horror and she would be confined to a wheelchair for the rest of her life.

Suddenly Jess was overcome with a crazy impulse.

She ran out of school and headed for home. She tried to look like a jogger so the shorts wouldn't be so much of a mystery. But it's hard to jog when you're wearing slip-on black shoes with a two-inch heel. Especially when you're carrying a heavy school bag. She knew she was getting into much worse trouble, bunking off like this. But she simply could not handle being undressed in public. She didn't care about the big trouble that would await her in school tomorrow. She just had to be reunited with her own clothes.

The journey home consisted of part jogging, part walking, a couple of rest stops when she sat gasping on convenient low walls, and a mad lurch when her heel turned over. But eventually Jess arrived at her own dear front door. She let herself in, dashed upstairs and dived into her beloved bedroom. Granny's door had been open when she whizzed past, and Granny came out and stood at the bottom of the stairs.

'Jess!' she called. 'Is that you? Or is it a burglar?'

'It's all right, it's a burglar!' Jess called back, ripping off Ben Jones's shorts and ransacking her lingerie drawer for a magic pair of knickers that would transport her straight to the centre of an extremely private rainforest on an undiscovered continent somewhere. Magic pants rather like the old Arabian carpet, only slightly more downmarket.

'Are you all right, dear?' called Granny.

'Yes, fine!' shouted Jess. 'I just slipped and got some mud on my skirt, so they told me to come home and get changed.'

'There's a terrible famine in Africa again!' said Granny. 'I'm going to send them part of my pension next week.'

As Jess struggled into a pair of soothing white cotton knicks and a short but sassy grey skirt, a huge wave of hunger ripped through her tum. She hoped the starving in Africa wouldn't mind if she went downstairs and made herself a cheese sandwich the size of Jupiter.

Jess went downstairs. She was relieved to discover she was still hungry. She knew that people with broken hearts were often unable to face beans on toast, but she was sure she could manage a double portion – with loads of grated cheese and a chocolate milkshake. Food was some comfort for the loss of her brilliant career.

All her plans for comedy celebrity with Fred had turned to dust and ashes. They had planned to start their brilliant career with a fortnight at the Edinburgh Festival Fringe, where they would be spotted by a TV executive in an Armani suit who would offer them a series. The T-shirts and the *Fred 'n' Jess* cereal promotion deals would surely follow. The house in Malibu, the apartment in Paris, the sleigh drawn down a snowy Fifth Avenue by a team of sturdy King Charles spaniels … all were revealed as a pathetic fantasy.

'Are you going back to school, dear?' said Granny, as Jess finished the last of her milkshake. 'Or would you like to watch a *Miss Marple* video with me? I'd like to see that one again – the one about the body in the library.'

Jess hesitated. She *so* needed to get back to school, to go straight to Mr Powell's office, fall face down on his carpet, and beg his forgiveness. That was the only sensible thing to do – her only hope of stopping the rot. Since the start of this term she had somehow got caught in an ever-tighter web of evil, like poor Frodo Baggins in the gigantic spider-thing's web in *The Lord of the Rings*.

But the thought of going back to school and confronting Mr Powell filled her with such absolute dread, she just couldn't face it. Not right now.

'No, it's OK, Granny,' said Jess. 'I'd love to see *Miss Marple* with you. I don't have to go back to school today because there's a – a staff meeting

121

to reorganise the timetable and they're letting us all off early.'

'Well, that is a stroke of luck,' said Granny. 'Let's have some hot chocolate, shall we?'

Though she was still bursting from her recent lunch, Jess could not but agree, and volunteered to make the hot choc while Granny went to find the video.

The kettle was almost boiling when the phone rang. Jess had grabbed it before she'd realised it would have been better to let it ring.

'Hello?' she said cautiously. She must not reveal her identity.

'Jess Jordan?' said a brisk man's voice.

'Er – yes,' said Jess, catastrophically unable to lie for the first time in months.

'This is Mr Powell. Why aren't you in school? You were supposed to come and see me. What's your explanation?'

Jess's heart jolted into a mad samba rhythm, and disastrously, the kettle came to the boil and emitted a long drawn-out wailing whistle. Jess reached out madly to turn the gas off, and somehow knocked the open jar of chocolate powder off the table. It flew through the air, scattering brown dust in all directions, before landing on Mum's slippers.

'I'm terribly sorry,' said Jess. 'But I slipped on the school field and got covered in mud, so I thought I'd better just quickly dash home and get changed, and when I arrived I discovered that my granny wasn't well.'

'Who's that on the phone, dear?' enquired Granny, perkily and healthily, from the doorway.

'It's all right, Granny, it's not about the ambulance,' said Jess, winking in what she hoped was a helpfully clear message: DON'T SAY ANOTHER WORD AND GET THE HELL OUT OF HERE.

'The *ambulance*, dear?'

'Yes, Granny. It won't be long. Go and lie down again. Sorry, Mr Powell, it's just that my granny doesn't feel at all well – she thinks she might be having a heart attack, so I called the ambulance. It'll be here in a minute.'

'Where are your parents?'

'My mum's at the library and my dad's in Cornwall.'

'Does your mother know what's happening?'

'Er …' Jess wasn't sure what the best answer would be. If her mother didn't know what was happening, it would make it even more important for Jess to stay at home looking after Granny. 'No,' she said, 'I tried to ring her at the library but I couldn't get through.'

'Don't worry,' said Mr Powell, in masterful Head of Year mode. 'I'll ring the library and tell her. Don't leave your grandmother. Keep her upright and loosen her clothing. And I want to see you in my office as soon as you are back at school.'

'Yes, of course,' said Jess.

Mr Powell put the phone down, no doubt to ring Jess's mum and break the dreadful news.

Jess ran through into Granny's room. She wasn't in the mood for *Miss Marple* right now. In fact she was so panicky and frazzled that for a split second she thought an ambulance really would be arriving in a few minutes.

'Why did you tell me to go and lie down?' asked Granny, looking rather cross.

'Granny,' said Jess, 'I've done a terrible thing.'

'What's that, dear?' Granny looked worried.

'I told a lie,' said Jess, unable to remember clearly which lie was which. 'That was Mr Powell, our Head of Year. I'm not supposed to be at home, you see. For some stupid reason I told him you weren't well. So I wouldn't have to go back to school today. I told him you thought you might be having a heart attack and we'd called an ambulance.'

Granny didn't say anything for a while. She was

124

obviously thinking.

'I'm really sorry, Granny,' Jess went on. 'But I got myself into a kind of silly mess. I really did get mud all over my skirt. I didn't mean to involve you.'

'The thing is, dear,' Granny spoke at last. Jess prayed that Granny would forgive, play ball, nay, agree to go along with the charade. Maybe she'd even be a real sport and pretend she'd had chest pain. Though actually calling a real ambulance might be going a bit too far. And – oh Lawdy! – Jess would have to ring the library right away, to tell her mum it was all a misunderstanding.

'It's a bit of a coincidence,' said Granny, looking rather embarrassed for once. 'I haven't been feeling all that well recently. In fact I've made an appointment to see the doctor this evening and I'd be very grateful if you'd come with me, dear, just to keep me company, you know, and hold my hand. And whatever you do, don't say anything to your mum.'

Jess's heart leapt in fear. For a moment it seemed as if she was the one who would be experiencing cardiac arrest. Granny was really ill! So ill she didn't want to mention it to Mum! Oh no! Jess was sure she was being punished for her terrible behaviour. *Please God*, she prayed urgently, *don't let Granny die!* It was such a long time since she had last prayed, though, that she was afraid God would be really cheesed off and send the Grim Reaper along anyway, just to spite her.

14

GAZE NOT FORBIDDENLY AT ADULT MOVIES: THE ZOO IS A BETTER SOURCE OF SEX EDUCATION

'Of course I will, Granny!' said Jess. 'You don't think it's your heart, do you? Maybe we should ring an ambulance anyway.'

'No, no, I don't want a blasted ambulance,' said Granny rather irritably. 'I want to watch *Miss Marple*. It's just a sort of giddy thing that happens sometimes. I don't want your mum to know because she's such a hypochondriac. She'll be looking it up on the blinking internet and telling me I've got some awful disease.'

'Right! Right!' said Jess. It was true, her mum did worry. In fact, she'd be worrying now – Jess simply *had* to ring the library. She raced into the kitchen and found the number, which was helpfully written on

127

the door of the fridge in Jess's childhood magnetic letters. It was spelt deliberately wrongly: **LIBRY**, because they hadn't been able to find any As. Jess dialled, and the phone rang for ages. Eventually somebody answered, in a quiet sort of library voice. Jess recognised Alison, Mum's colleague.

'Alison – it's Jess! Can I speak to Mum, please?'

'Oh Jess – she's just gone – she had a message that your granny's had a heart attack.'

'No, no, it's OK! I was with Granny and she feels much better now so we've cancelled the ambulance!'

'Well, don't worry, dear – she'll be home in a minute,' said Alison.

'But there's no need for her to come! Granny's fine!'

'Maybe you should ring her mobile, then,' said Alison. 'I'm so glad everything's all right. I've got to go, Jess – we're terribly short-staffed today.'

Jess went back into Granny's room. Granny had started the video and was watching various trailers for other whodunnits.

'Mum's coming home,' she said. Granny looked alarmed.

'What for?'

'Mr Powell rang and told her you'd had a heart

attack,' said Jess.

'What? What? I've lost track of it all!' said Granny.

'It was my fault,' said Jess. 'I'm afraid I got into a bit of a tangle. I kind of panic when I'm cornered and I say the first thing that comes into my head.'

'Ring her mobile, dear, and tell her I'm perfectly OK,' said Granny. 'I don't want to bother her, and *Miss Marple*'s starting now, look.'

The cosy signature tune of *Miss Marple* wafted across the room, suggesting country lanes, gossipy villages, and people getting stabbed suddenly in areas of outstanding natural beauty. Jess ran back to the kitchen and dialled Mum's mobile. She got the answering service. Mum always switched her mobile off when she was driving. There was nothing to do but wait and watch *Miss Marple* until Mum came home.

They were just into the first appearance of the sinister lesbians when the front door opened and Mum rushed in.

'Mum!' she cried, kneeling by Granny's chair and grabbing her hand. 'Are you OK? What happened?'

'Nothing, dear,' said Granny placidly. 'I'm fine. It was a misunderstanding.'

'What do you mean?' cried Mum, evidently irritated as well as relieved.

'It wasn't a *complete* misunderstanding, Granny,' said Jess. 'You did have a bad chest pain, and I was just about to phone the ambulance when Mr Powell rang.'

'But what was Mr Powell doing, ringing you?' asked Mum. 'And why are you at home?'

'Oh,' said Jess, trying to sound immensely casual and accomplished, 'I slipped on the school field and got covered in mud, so I came home to change. Mr Powell was just checking I was OK because ...' she hesitated, '... of that girl who went out of school and met –'

Suddenly the phone rang, and Mum went out to answer it. Phew! Jess had a few minutes to try and improve her story. On the other hand, what if it was Mr Powell on the phone again, or even worse, Miss Thorn? Then Mum would get to hear the ghastly truth about Jess's career of crime. But beyond the soundtrack of the video, Jess could hear her mum on the phone – and she was *giggling*!

It obviously wasn't Mr Powell or Miss Thorn. What a relief. But who the hell was it? Mum almost never giggled on the phone. The sound was unusual and alarming.

'What a lovely idea!' Mum was saying. 'Thank you so much! I'd love to! ... Yes, fine. After the lesson.

Yes, come early … See you tonight then, Nori.'

Ah. It was her Japanese pupil. Mum came back into the sitting room, looking kind of flushed and happy.

'Nori's asked me out to have some sushi tonight, after the lesson,' she said. 'If you don't mind? There's a casserole in the freezer you could have – I'll get it out now to defrost.'

No mention of the heart attack crisis. The phone call from Nori seemed to have wiped everything from Mum's mind. This was convenient. She went into the kitchen and got the casserole out, then came back into the sitting room.

'I love *Miss Marple*,' she said, sitting on the arm of the sofa. 'I wish I could stay and watch it with you instead of going back to the library.'

'Yes, Mum, stay!' said Jess, pulling her arm. 'Let's *all* bunk off.'

'You're not bunking off, are you?' said Mum, looking suddenly shocked.

'Of course not!' said Jess. 'It was just a joke! Mr Powell knew all about me coming home. In fact he suggested I should go home and change. And when he found out that Granny had heart pain, he told me not to leave her alone. So I'd better not go back to school today. Although of course Granny's

131

fine, as you can see. It was just a burp, wasn't it, Granny?'

'What was, dear?' Granny had got caught up again with *Miss Marple* and was watching a woman loitering suspiciously by some flowerbeds.

'Nothing, just your so-called heart pain,' said Jess, giving Granny a sly dig with her elbow. 'You just had that massive burp, and it all went away, didn't it?'

'Oh yes, dear. I should never have trusted those pickles,' said Granny, not taking her eyes off the screen for an instant.

Having been assured that Granny was not really ill, Mum went back to work. She seemed to think it was OK for Jess to stay at home, as long as she 'made up the work tomorrow'. Ha! Poor deluded soul. Little did Mum know that Jess still hadn't made up the work she'd missed from way back last *year*.

Jess felt quite exhausted by the frenzied bout of lying she'd had to do, so she drank about a pint of Coke, curled up on the sofa cuddling Granny and tried to tune in to *Miss Marple*. But though usually she loved nothing better than to follow the exploits of the brilliant old sleuth, today she just couldn't concentrate.

All the ingredients of her massive crisis kept swirling round and round in her head: the two most frightening teachers in school baying for her blood! And darling old Fred, looking at her as if she was something unpleasant on the pavement.

Later she and Granny shared a cheese omelette with salad, and Jess drank another pint of Coke. Then they watched a whole new *Miss Marple*. Jess was half-asleep by now, but making plans. A bit later she would ring Flora. She'd call her on her mobile, after school. She simply had to pour out her heart.

In fact, she would invite Flora round and they could have a heart-to-heart up in her room, with Nirvana providing the soundtrack. Oh no! Wait! Jess was supposed to be escorting Granny to the doctor's this evening. Never mind, she and Flora could have a telephone heart-to-heart instead.

Miss Marple solved the crime, and Jess drank another huge glass of Coke (was she addicted or something? Possibly). Then she nipped to the kitchen and dialled Flora's number. *Answer it, answer it*, she breathed. She just had to talk to Flo. If she didn't, she would burst.

'Hi, babe!' said Flora. 'Are you OK? Where did you disappear to after the fabulous pants show?'

'Oh, I just bunked off home,' said Jess. 'I didn't fancy seeing Mr Powell before his lunch. You know he's a major carnivore. How are you? Everything OK?'

She always tried to be polite. However, she was preparing to download her epic tale of disaster as soon as Flora had said she was OK.

'OK – fantastic!' said Flora. 'Guess what?'

'What?' This was slightly irritating. This wasn't on the agenda.

'I've got a part in *Twelfth Night*!'

'No! Fantastic! Congrats, old bean!'

'And guess what? I've got Viola!'

'Viola! The lead role, brilliant! You'll be brilliant!' said Jess, trying to ignore a terrible wave of cold jealousy which was rising up her legs off the kitchen floor.

'And guess what!'

Jess was a bit tired of all this guessing.

'What?'

'Jack Stevens is playing Orsino! So I'll have lots of rehearsals with just him and me! I can't wait!'

'How completely fabulous. I'm thrilled for you!' said Jess. But secretly she was gutted. She couldn't spoil Flora's high by starting to drone on tragically about her own problems, could she?

'Gotta go now, babe,' said Flora suddenly. 'I'm running out of charge. I'm meeting my mum in town for a celebration tea at Luigi's!'

'Cheers, enjoy!' said Jess.

That was it, then. Jess trudged dolefully up to her room and prepared to spend the evening wallowing in lonely misery. She kind of half wanted to go to the loo, but she was so miserable, it seemed like too much of an effort.

She was halfway through the first wave of tragic despair when her mum came home, rushed upstairs and locked herself in the bathroom. This was annoying. Jess had been planning to have a pee in a moment or two. She must have drunk about six pints of Coke today.

'Mum!' She hammered on the door. 'I want a pee!'

'Use the outside loo!' called Mum. 'I'm having a quick shower! Nori will be here any minute!'

What disastrous timing! Jess ran downstairs. The outside loo was primitive beyond words. They had plans to convert it and the adjoining coal shed into a swish new bathroom for Granny, but they hadn't managed to raise the necessary cash yet. So it was basically just a rather smelly outside loo where lots of horrid spiders lived.

Granny used it sometimes in the daytime if she couldn't face the stairs. In fact – oh no! She was in there *right now*.

'Granny!' called Jess, increasingly desperate. 'Sorry to disturb you, but will you be long?'

'I'm afraid I might be some time, dear,' said Granny. 'I've been wrestling with my lazy bowel all day, and I want to get it sorted before we go to the doctor's.'

'Say no more!' said Jess, adding a silent *please*. 'I'll go upstairs, don't worry. Relax!'

There was only one thing for it. She was going to have to pee *in her own back garden*. She ventured down towards the picnic table. It was shaded by a couple of trees and fairly secluded down there – but only fairly. The windows of all the neighbouring houses were sort of looking down at her. Jess edged behind a bush near the picnic table, and pretended to have dropped something. She bent down and peeped up to see if anyone was watching. It seemed nobody was.

Swiftly she pulled down her pants and let rip. But, horror! As she peered through the leaves towards the house, she saw the back door swing open. What? Mum was in the shower, Granny was in the outside loo – who the hell was it? Jess watched in helpless horror as *Mr Nishizawa* came out into the garden! He headed down the path for the picnic table right next to where Jess was still having the longest pee in the history of urination. Any minute now he would catch sight of her! What could she do?

15

COMMIT NOT GROSS ACTS
IN PUBLIC WITH A
DOUBLE BURGER AND FRIES

Jess reckoned she had about five seconds to act. In a flash she realised that it wouldn't be the standing up that was the problem – it would be the pulling up of the pants that gave the game away. So with one deft move she cut short the pee (in itself a major physical triumph), stepped right out of her pants and sort of kicked them under the bush, while surging upwards, tugging her skirt down and producing a glamorous and confident smile.

Mr Nishizawa was looking at her. She wasn't completely sure whether he had seen her peeing or not. Thank God he was Japanese. They were the most polite people in the world and she was sure he wouldn't mention it. And anyway, he didn't have the necessary vocabulary.

'Good evening!' said Mr Nishizawa, bowing and smiling. 'Door is open – ring bell, nobody answer. Look for teacher in garden.'

'That's fine, OK, terrific!' said Jess. 'I was just looking for herbs – you know!'

He looked puzzled. She picked a piece off the nearest bush and sniffed it in rapture. He smiled and bowed again. *This is what it must be like to be the Queen*, thought Jess. *People bowing all the time*. Although she doubted if the Queen had ever been caught short and had to pee behind a bush in her own garden.

This thought made Jess laugh out loud, but because it seemed rather mad to do so, she turned it into a kind of Moment of Rapture.

'Ha ha! Hee hee! The garden looks so fabulous at this time of year!' she cried, tossing the handful of leaves in the air with crazy joy.

'Garden – beautiful!' agreed Mr Nishizawa.

'Come on – I'll tell Mum you're here!' said Jess.

Mr Nishizawa bowed yet again (what an elastic back that guy must have) and indicated that she should go first.

Jess accepted, and led the way back to the house. She was becoming rather anxious about the shortness of her skirt, since she was, for the first time in her life, without any underpants in public.

There was only one step up into the house, thank goodness, and just before she climbed it, she turned round to Mr Nishizawa and said, 'Do you think it'll rain? Look at that cloud!' and made a sweeping gesture towards the sky. Mr Nishizawa obligingly looked up over his shoulder, so he missed what might have been a cheeky flash of Jess's lower buttock as she skipped up the step.

Jess and Mr Nishizawa walked through the kitchen and into the hall. Granny suddenly appeared from behind them. She had finished in the outside loo and was already wearing her coat and carrying her bag.

'Oh hello, dear!' said Granny to Mr Nishizawa. She'd never attempted to pronounce his name.

'Good evening!' he said, bowing.

'I've given up on my silly old bowel, dear,' Granny went on in an undertone to Jess. 'Now come on – we must go, it'll take us ten minutes to get there.' Jess nodded. She wanted desperately to go upstairs and get a pair of pants. But how could she, with Mr Nishizawa and Granny standing in the hall and staring up the stairs? If she went upstairs now, they'd get the kind of view normally only available in rather sordid nightclubs.

'Granny – do you want to take Mr Nishizawa into the sitting room so he can wait there?'

140

'Never mind all that, dear. Your mum will be down in a minute – Madeleine!' bawled Granny. 'Your pupil's here!'

'OK!' shouted Mum from the bathroom. 'Coming!'

'Would you like to wait in the sitting room, Mr Nishizawa?' asked Jess.

Mr Nishizawa bowed. 'Rain a lot in England. Rain also in Japan much time.' He was really rather cute. All the same, Jess couldn't help wishing he could be wafted right back to Japan immediately, on a pillar of fire. At least until she'd got her underwear sorted.

'Your mother very good teacher!' Mr Nishizawa smiled and stood gazing up the stairs, impatient to see the vision descending: his honoured and revered teacher.

'Come on, dear, we must go,' said Granny, heading for the door. 'I hate being late for the doctor.'

Jess had only two choices: she could either go upstairs now and show her bare bum to Mr Nishizawa (and, less crucially, to Granny), or she could accompany Granny on a trip to the doctor's, wearing no pants at all.

Mr Nishizawa smiled with great politeness. There was no contest. Jess was going to have to leave the house bare-assed.

Out in the street, she took Granny's arm. Granny was blathering on about all the people she'd known who had had bits of their bodies cut off. And in each case, the amputation had been preceded by a visit to the doctor.

But Jess was barely listening. Or rather, she was barely not-listening. The bareness of her bum was her only concern. This was like some appalling living nightmare. Her skirt was, she calculated, about four inches above the knee. This meant that, as long as she stayed bolt upright, nobody should see anything embarrassing.

Jess silently thanked God that she wasn't wearing a skirt in a light material, or with playful pleats that would flicker in the slightest breeze. Instead, it was a rather dull grey school-type skirt. Jess remembered turning it up secretly, taking four inches off its length, sewing away laboriously, determined to have a skirt that was nearly illegal according to school rules. She was being punished for it now.

Just keep my bum discreetly veiled from the general public, Lord, she prayed silently, *and I will never wear a miniskirt again. I will only wear ankle-length skirts or possibly a whole robe in the Biblical manner.*

'Mrs Chideock had to have a breast off,' said Granny, with a sad sigh. 'And I knew a chap once who'd lost a leg in the war, and strangely enough, his wife lost a leg too, because of circulatory problems.'

'How awful!' said Jess. A number of extremely tasteless jokes cropped up cheekily in her mind, but she was sure they were the work of Satan, and she refused even to think of them in case God was watching.

A woman was walking towards them holding a small child's hand on one side and a dog on a lead on the other. Ever since they had left the house, Jess had been dreading the approach of small animals. What if the small child looked up at the wrong moment? What if the dog jumped up for an impudent sniff?

Dogs were so awful about that sniffing business. Just because they loved sniffing each other's bottoms didn't mean they could take liberties with the human race. Jess had once been hoisted right up into the air by the nose of a German shepherd who had taken a fancy to the seat of her jeans.

'I'll just change sides, if you don't mind, Granny,' said Jess, hastily going round the other side of Granny and taking her arm nearest to the road. 'I'm a little bit scared of dogs, to be honest.'

'But it's only a little one,' said Granny.

'The little ones are the worst,' said Jess.

The woman walked past without mishap. Jess uttered another silent prayer of thanks.

143

'Then,' Granny resumed her catalogue of amputees, 'I knew a woman once who lost a finger in a circus. She was holding a horse by the harness and when she let it go, the harness got caught in her ring. She was quite all right, though. Those surgeons can do wonders these days.'

'Don't worry, then, Granny,' said Jess. 'If you've been feeling dizzy, I expect the doctor'll just cut off your head, and you'll be fine and dandy.'

Granny laughed. Luckily she had a very macabre sense of humour.

They arrived at the doctor's and Jess thanked God again that the surgery was on the ground floor. But when they arrived in the waiting room, her blood ran cold. They would obviously have to sit down. And what happens when you sit down? Your skirt rides up! Disastrously, sometimes.

And then when you get up again … Jess had frequently observed girls wearing miniskirts getting up from a sitting position. And basically what happened was that frequently you got a flash of knickers. And if there were no knickers, well, Jess couldn't bear to think of what might happen.

'I'll stand up, Granny,' she said, after Granny had checked in. 'You go and sit over there.' Luckily there weren't many seats available. The waiting room was, as usual, crowded. People all sitting rather too close together and a horrid embarrassed atmosphere.

Jess went over and stood with her back to the wall. Granny sat down, sighed and smiled. Then her beady little eyes caught sight of the magazines on a low coffee table just out of reach, in the middle of the room.

'Pass me one of those magazines, will you, Jess, love?' said Granny. For a moment Jess felt that, though she loved her granny passionately, decapitation could not come a moment too soon. In order to pass her the magazine, she would have to bend down, offering a glorious view of her arse to the people seated behind her, pick up the magazine, and then bend down again to offer it to Granny – exposing herself all over again. A kind of encore.

Jess fell to her knees as if about to pray. Some people looked a bit startled. Then she sort of shuffled to the coffee table on her knees, keeping her back bolt upright. Making sure her heels were clamping her skirt safely up against her buttocks, she reached forward stiffly, like a marionette, picked up a magazine by the corner, and threw it to Granny, who fumbled. Of course, it fell on the floor.

'Oh dear, I'm so sorry, love,' said Granny. 'Pick it up, would you?'

Now the whole roomful of people was watching in

amusement. Jess hesitated. One or two women exchanged looks which meant 'Blinking teenagers! Too lazy to get out of their own way!'

'Sorry, Granny,' said Jess. 'I've ricked my back really badly and I can't bend over.'

A man sitting next to Granny bent over and picked up the magazine. Jess silently asked God to forgive most of that man's sins immediately and reserve a specially comfy cloud for him in heaven. Granny received the magazine with a gracious smile.

Jess also picked up a magazine. Just because she was marooned on the carpet, sitting on her feet, wearing a short skirt and no panties, didn't mean she couldn't catch up with what the celebs were doing. She was planning to wait until everybody else had gone before getting up. Until then she would just kneel here reading *Hello!* magazine. *OK*, she thought, *my situation is majorly ghastly. But it could be a lot worse.* And that was the moment when Fred walked in.

16

LIE NOT ON THE SOFA ALL DAY BUT GET UP OFF THY BUM AND WALK. EVEN IF IT'S JUST TO THE FRIDGE

Fred's eyes kind of flared when he saw her, and he blushed. Granny looked up and gave a little cry of pleasure.

'Oh Fred!' she said. 'How are you, dear? I haven't seen you for a day or two.'

'Er, fine, thanks,' said Fred, and hesitated. There was only one empty chair. On one side of it there was a woman holding a struggling, whimpering baby and on the other side there was an old man who looked as if he might be the source of a rather unpleasant smell. No wonder nobody had sat there.

Fred checked himself in at reception, naturally avoided the empty chair and instead sort of sauntered over to a fishtank and leant on the wall next to it. He glanced briefly in, as if he wanted to make sure there was nothing in the tank which might cause a horrid surprise – a small but turbo-charged shark, for instance – and then he looked back into the room, and somehow his eyes kind of got caught on Jess's. Her heart turned over. Fred looked as if he was just about to say something to her, when Granny spoke again.

'What's wrong with you, Fred, love? What's a healthy young man like you doing in the doctor's surgery?'

Jess cringed anew. Granny ought to know that you never ask people in a doctor's waiting room what's wrong with them. It might be something really embarrassing. Though nothing could be quite as embarrassing as what Jess was suffering from – a shortage of underwear.

'Oh,' said Fred, switching into his usual style, 'where to begin? My elbows don't quite match, for a start, and my toes have turned purple.' A fat girl in the corner giggled. Jess made plans to kill her immediately. 'But my main trouble,' Fred went on, 'is pain in my rollerblades.'

'Oh, I had pain in my rollerblades once,' said Granny. 'It was too much gardening.' A few people smiled. Jess made plans to kill them immediately.

'Shoulder blades, you mean, Granny!' said Jess.

'Yes, well, it was when I had a greenhouse,' said Granny, getting all nostalgic. 'I used to stand there for hour after hour, sowing seeds in pots, you know, dear. I had over three hundred pots one year.'

There was a slight pause. Fred looked at Jess. There was a horrible public, embarrassed look on his face.

'How's Jim's boil?' a middle-aged woman said suddenly to an old lady beside her.

'It's burst now, thank God,' said the old lady. There was another silence. Fred looked at Jess, and there was desperation in his eyes.

'Have you two been writing any more of your comedy routines for that Christmas Show at school?' asked Granny, looking from Jess to Fred and back. How dare Granny reveal the secrets of her private life to this whole room of people! Jess made plans to kill her immediately.

'Oh, there isn't going to be a show this year,' said Fred. 'There's going to be a production of *Twelfth Night* instead.'

'Oh, lovely, dear,' said Granny. 'And are you going to be in it?'

Fred hesitated and gulped. 'Well, yes, I am,' he said. 'But I don't think Jess is.' He hesitated, and looked at Jess again.

'I didn't audition for it, Granny,' said Jess. 'I hate Shakespeare.'

A woman appeared at the doctors' door and called Granny's name. There were several doctors at this practice and Granny appeared to have struck lucky and had hardly had to wait at all.

'Oh, that's me!' she said, getting up. 'I won't be long, dear,' she smiled to Jess, and trotted off to her appointment.

A silence spread through the room. Fred looked at Jess and pulled a face – a kind of God-isn't-this-a-nightmare sort of face. Jess shrugged and did a kind of false smile, the sort the Prime Minister does when he is trying to pretend he isn't hurt by newspaper reports that he is more unpopular than ever.

'Why aren't you wearing the football shorts?' asked Fred suddenly. Everybody in the room looked at Jess's thighs. She blushed comprehensively. She made plans to kill Fred at the earliest opportunity. How dare he make fun of her in front of everybody?

'Oh God, if only I was, you've no idea,' she said. Then silently, in her heart of hearts, she uttered one of her most hysterical silent prayers. *Dear God, I know I've begged you to rescue me from awful situations before, but this has got to be the worst yet: being tormented in public by the person who has broken my heart, whilst wearing no pants and sitting on my feet, which have pins and needles. Please God, get me out of this and I promise I will never tell a lie again. And I mean it this time! Please God – send a miracle. A power cut or something. Just a minor miracle will do.*

Moments after she finished her prayer, the struggling baby was sick all over the smelly old man. In the ensuing fracas, Jess kind of scuttled away on her knees into a corner, surged to her feet and escaped out to the lobby. Following a blind instinct to seek shelter, Jess rushed down a corridor where she knew there was a loo. She plunged in and locked the door behind her. A loo had never been more welcome. Not for its toilet facilities, but for its privacy. Jess would never leave. She would refuse to come out. She would live here for ever.

Then she noticed something. A mac was hanging from a row of pegs. It was a navy blue mac. And it looked nice and long. Jess tried it on. Oh joy! Oh bliss! It went right down to her knees!

God, you are ace! she whispered. *You are Numero Uno! I shall never wear short skirts again, as well as not telling lies!*

However, there was the slight problem that it was not her mac. There was, of course, the larger problem that it was navy blue – normally a colour which Jess would rather die than wear. No matter. She would endure any kind of style horror rather than feel the cold early autumn air on her buttocks for a moment longer.

She opened the door and peeped out. There was nobody about. She peered round the corner of the waiting room. She would ask Fred to tell Granny she was waiting for her outside. But Fred wasn't in the waiting room any more. Evidently he had gone in to see the doc.

Hastily Jess walked out – right out, into the car park. She sat down on a low wall facing the back door of the Health Centre. When Granny came out, she would see her straight away. Jess just hoped that the owner of the mac didn't come out and recognise it. It was so damned comforting, sitting on fabric again. She would never take her pants off in future, in this life or the next.

She put her hand in her pocket and felt something unusual – something plastic, like a pen. She looked at it. What was it? Oh no – it was a thermometer in a kind of case! She had possibly stolen a *nurse's* mac! Dear God, was there any end to this torment? She wondered whether she would get sent to prison if she was caught, and, strangely, she didn't really mind. In fact, if a life of freedom was what she had been putting up with for the past few days, she hoped her sentence would be as long as possible.

17

ALWAYS CALL HOME
IF OUT LATE LEST THY PARENTS
GO APESHIT WITH WORRY

Someone was coming out. Help! *It was a nurse!* She was all kitted out in that nurse-style dress – in matching navy blue. Perhaps this was her *very own mac* Jess had stolen! She headed straight for Jess with a purposeful look on her face: determined, perhaps, to seize the mac and call the police. Jess's heart started to thud. Although maybe, if she became a glamorous local criminal and was put on probation, Fred would want to go out with her again.

But perhaps not. And as the nurse covered the last few yards, Jess cringed with horror. Her blood froze. She prepared a preposterous story about thinking the mac was hers. *Dear God*, she said, *I know I promised you I'd never lie again if you got me out of that waiting room alive, but could we start from, say, half an hour's time?*

'Lovely weather!' said the nurse with a brisk smile, and walked past Jess.

'Mmmm! Wonderful!' agreed Jess in a parody of relaxed late summerhood. The nurse unlocked her car, which was parked just behind Jess, and drove off to deliver more babies or dress more wounds, or fiddle with old people's feet, or whatever nurses did.

Jess was reeling from the sheer terror of her role as possessor of stolen goods. Perhaps even walking home bare-assed was preferable to a life of crime. And if she was detected and arrested and taken to the police station, and searched – imagine policefolk knowing you were without pants! It might even count as another offence. Jess decided to take the mac back right now. She was sure God would approve.

So she got up off the wall and strolled back into the Health Centre. Once inside the doors she turned left into a long corridor. The loos were about halfway down, on the left. All she had to do was reach the ladies' loo before she was challenged by any nurse, and replace the mac. Great! The corridor was empty.

But seconds later somebody appeared at the other end. It was Fred. Jess flinched. Just how much hassle could be fitted into one day? No, wait, this was her chance to utter those few common-sense words

155

which would miraculously restore her relationship with him.

They locked eyes as they walked towards each other and met, predictably, right by the door of the loo.

'So,' said Jess, trying to sound jaunty and delightful, though her heart was being chewed by invisible mad dogs, 'how's things?'

These were not the few magic words she had planned. Fred shrugged and looked down at her, but he did not make the soft owly hooting noise which was part of their secret understanding. He looked as if she was someone he saw occasionally in the café.

'Oh, couldn't be better,' he said. And then he looked up and down the corridor as if wishing to escape. 'How's things with you?'

'Fantastic!' said Jess, ignoring the pangs of misery. 'I'm having the best time. So you're in *Twelfth Night*. What part are you playing?'

'Malvolio,' said Fred. 'I'll just spend all my time sneering at people and being humiliated.'

'No change there, then,' said Jess.

'Why didn't you audition?' asked Fred. 'I somehow expected you to be there on the list. A serving wench perhaps, or grieving countess.'

'Oh, I didn't fancy it,' said Jess. 'I'm planning a

comedy show, just like we always used to have. Sketches and maybe a couple of musical numbers.'

Fred's face changed. For a split second he looked really shocked.

'What, do you mean you're doing it on your own?' he said. 'You are of course famous for your powers of organisation, but –'

'I expect I'll find somebody to help,' said Jess crisply. 'You'll be too busy, I take it?'

Fred frowned. A pulse was racing in his neck.

'Well, I suppose I will be a bit busy,' he said. 'The rehearsal schedule is quite terrifying. But, you know, if I can help in any small way – distributing leaflets, whatever – nearer the time ... Assassinating Thorn ...'

'Thanks, yeah, whatever,' said Jess, trying not to sound crushed. Then she had an idea. 'Never mind about the comedy show,' she said. 'You can do something to help me, right now.'

'What?' said Fred, looking rather panicky.

'It's nothing illegal,' said Jess. 'Just lend me your jacket for an hour.'

Fred hesitated. He even frowned slightly. Then he shrugged, took his jacket off, and handed it over to her. It was a grey marl hoodie thing.

'This new fetish about men's clothing can be cured, you know,' he said.

157

'Thanks!' said Jess. 'You'll never know how grateful I am.'

She darted into the ladies' loo, hung up the nurse's mac, tied Fred's jacket around her waist by the arms so it hung down and hid her bum, and then carefully inspected her face in the mirror. Oh no! She looked like a deranged ape.

Never mind. Now was her chance. This time she really would say the magic words. She rehearsed it with what she hoped was an attractive pout. *Fred, I don't know how we ever got into this misunderstanding, but let's get rid of it right now and go back to how we were in the summer.*

She plucked up her courage and opened the door. Oh no! Granny had arrived and was chatting friskily to Fred.

'Hello, dear!' she said to Jess. 'I was just telling Fred the doctor thinks it's nothing serious, just my ageing neck.'

'Oh good, Granny, thank goodness!' Jess squeezed her arm.

'Yes – er, well – must be going,' said Fred, backing off. 'Got to feed my iguana or he gets restless.'

'Has Fred really got an iguana, dear?' asked Granny as they walked home.

'No,' said Jess. 'It was just a kind of joke.'

158

She sighed. It seemed such a long time since she had been to Fred's house – even though it was only a few days. Would she ever go there again? Possibly not.

'Is everything all right between you and Fred, love?' asked Granny suddenly, with evident telepathic insight.

'Oh yes, Granny – just fine,' said Jess. She was so tempted to break down sobbing on Granny's shoulder and pour out all her woes, but it wouldn't be fair. Granny was positively skittish now she knew her moments of wooziness were just due to her ageing neck. It would be so unfair to pour out woes. It would be like tipping a lorry load of pig manure over the dear old lady. For the time being at least, it was Jess's duty to bear her sorrows alone.

Besides, she really did have one or two things to look forward to. As soon as they arrived home, she would be able to put on a pair of knickers. This was a pleasure she would never underestimate again. Only those who have gone pantless in public will understand.

And beyond the great joy of being reunited with her lingerie, there was the delightful prospect of her interview with Mr Powell first thing in the morning.

There was, however, one really intriguing

possibility which might, heaven knows, lead to something truly earth-shattering. How was she going to get Fred's jacket back to him? Would it provide the excuse for the longed-for reconciliation? Would Fred sweep her into his arms once again? Right now she only had his sleeves wrapped round her. But it was a start.

18

PIERCE NOT THY FACE
NOR INSERT METAL
OBJECTS THEREIN

Once they got home, Jess waited till Granny was safely settled with a cup of tea in front of an old episode of the *X-Files*. Then she rang Fred on his mobile. It was switched off and she was invited to leave a message. She chickened out. It would take all evening to draft a message eloquent and witty enough to win his heart and restore their relationship to the bliss they had enjoyed in the summer. Jess knew if she tried to leave a message now, she would only stutter, croak and possibly choke.

OK, so his mobile was switched off. It so often was. Fred constantly forgot to charge it, or lost it under piles of DVDs. She would ring his landline instead. She didn't want to go round to his house without any warning. She'd done that a few times in the past and been turned away by Fred's dad, who reacted badly to any interruption of his diet of TV football and always assumed Fred was not at home.

Fred's mum answered the phone. Jess made a huge effort to sound frothy, lighthearted and devil-may-care.

'Oh hi! This is Jess. Is Fred in?'

'No, sorry, Jess – he came in a while ago and just went straight out again. He may have gone to Tom's.'

'Fine! Thanks! I'll try him there!'

Jess rang off trying to sound cheery, though her heart sank. Fred was becoming more and more elusive. A couple of stupid tears broke from her eyes and trailed down her cheeks. And then the doorbell rang.

Her heart leapt. It must be Fred! She panicked. She had to get rid of the tracks of her tears.

'Can you get that, please, Granny?' she called. 'I really need the loo!'

She raced upstairs, locked herself in the bathroom, and removed the salty streaks of mascara from her cheeks. Then Granny shouted up the stairs.

'It's what's his name come to pick up the thingumajig he lent you!'

Jess's heart performed a massive bounce and her face, in the bathroom mirror, glowed briefly like a lightbulb that has just been switched on.

'Show him in, Granny!' she yelled. 'I'll be down in a minute!'

Hastily she repaired her lipstick, and ladled a bit more mascara on to her lashes. Then, looking remarkably fabulous considering what a dire day she had had, she raced downstairs. He had come round! He wanted to make it up with her!

'He's in the kitchen, dear,' said Granny, returning to the TV to resume her feast of alien murder. Jess blew Granny a kiss and waltzed straight into the kitchen with a ravishing smile.

It was Ben. Jess tried not to let her smile fade, but she had to crank it up like mad to hide her disappointment.

'Ben!' she said. 'Great to see you!'

Her voice kind of cracked just slightly, so you could tell she was surprised and not expecting him. His blue eyes darkened for a split second. Though not an intellectual powerhouse, he was sensitive and perceptive and had seen and understood. And been hurt.

'Yeah, sorry to – um, disturb you, but could I have my – er – shorts and my jacket back?'

'Oh God! Of course!' said Jess. She felt so sorry for him, and so guilty about showing him her disappointment, that she felt she must make amends.

'I'll go and get them in a min. But first, how about a Coke? And there's some Doritos and a dip in that cupboard.'

'Cheers,' said Ben. He turned and opened the food cupboard – with the grace of an angel, as usual. Jess poured the Cokes out.

'See what's in the fridge,' she said. Actually, it felt really nice to be relaxing and having a bit of a snack with Ben, even if he wasn't Fred. In a way it was a relief. If he'd been Fred, there would have been major trauma and melodrama and frankly, Jess was so totally shattered by the Day from Hell, she didn't think she could handle any more of that kind of stuff right now.

'You've got feta cheese and olive dip,' said Ben. 'And – hey! – guacamole.'

'Great!' said Jess. 'I am almost clinically starving.'

'So tell me,' said Ben, 'what happened after I lent you the shorts? Flora said you'd disappeared.'

'Oh, just a routine bit of truancy,' said Jess with a shrug. 'Somehow I couldn't face my hot date with Irritable Powell so I thought I'd just postpone it till tomorrow.'

Ben laughed. 'You've got to see Powell? Bad luck.'

'Yes. I have been majorly bad. Miss Thorn and I

164

are bitter enemies and she sent me to him as a human sacrifice.'

'God, you've got so much – y'know, like, bottle,' he said. 'Joking about it. I'm, like, totally terrified of him.'

'Well, he's going to eat me alive tomorrow morning,' said Jess, 'so let's enjoy my last evening on earth. Pass the guacamole, Mr Jones.'

'How's everything, then?' asked Ben. 'You were – kind of, you know – a bit down earlier.'

'I have bounced back!' said Jess, trying hard to make it feel true. 'I'm determined to do this comedy show thing on my own. Flora and Fred won't be able to be in it though, because they're in *Twelfth Night*.'

'I'll help, if you like,' said Ben. 'Though I'm, uhh, total rubbish onstage. I could help backstage though. Organising stuff.'

'Ben! You're a gem!' said Jess. 'But that's crap about you being rubbish on stage. I know you'd be totally fabulous. I could write some sketches just for you. Maybe we could get Mackenzie in on it, too.' But even as she said this, Jess felt a dark crowd of misgivings gather about her heart. Ben was certainly not a natural actor or performer, except on the football field. And Mackenzie was such a control freak. He had gone out with Flora once and she'd said he was even more bossy than her dad.

They talked for a bit about the show, and how various other people might be interested in joining in. Though Jess had a kind of funny feeling of jealousy, as if she wanted to keep her show private for herself and Fred, and possibly Flora. But she agreed with everything Ben said because the conversation seemed to be taking place a long way away, somehow, and she didn't really care about anything any more.

'Well,' said Ben eventually, when they had finished the guacamole, 'I suppose I'd better go.'

'Your clothes!' said Jess. 'Won't be a min.' She ran upstairs and entered her room. Ben's jacket was right there on the bed, but for a panicky moment she couldn't see the shorts anywhere. The floor was covered with several rough heaps of clothing. It looked like a scale model of the Rockies.

She was just looking under her bed when she heard the front doorbell ring. Typical.

'Get that, will you!' she shouted. Ah! There were Ben's shorts, far away under the bed, right up against the skirting board. They must have fallen down the space between the bed and the wall. She crawled right under the bed and grabbed them, reversing out on her tummy and picking up loads of fluff and dust on the way.

Never mind. She really didn't care what she looked like. She'd found the jacket and the shorts. They looked in reasonable shape – not crumpled or anything. Thank God for synthetic materials. Jess left her bedroom, strolled to the top of the stairs, and then gasped and nearly fell to her death with shock. Three people stood in the hall looking up at her: Ben, Granny and Fred.

'Fred's come for his jacket, too, love,' said Granny. 'What's all this interest in men's clothes? Are you turning into a whatyamacallit?'

'I do hope so,' said Jess. 'Life as a whatyamacallit would be a lot less stressful, I'm sure.'

Her only consolation was that she was wearing pants. But she knew that, essential though it was, mere underwear could not rescue her from the intense emotional crisis that was about to engulf her.

19

PLUCK NOT THY EYEBROWS UNTIL THEY ARE INVISIBLE YEA, ONLY THE STRAGGLY BITS

She threw Ben's jacket and shorts down to him. He caught them. Fred's eyes flared with sudden understanding.

'Ah, so they were your shorts Jess was wearing this morning,' he said. Ben grinned and shrugged but somehow failed to find the necessary words to continue the conversation.

'Ben rescued me from a ghastly mud crisis on the school field,' said Jess. 'He happened to be passing as I wallowed in slime and offered his football shorts as a temporary solution.'

'I thought you looked very dashing in them,' said Fred. 'You should wear shorts more often. As an ironic fashion statement, of course.' There was a bitter look on his face.

'Isn't it funny how shorts go up and down?' pondered Granny, oblivious to the tension in the hall. 'I remember when I was a child, football players all wore shorts down to their knees. Then in the 1970s shorts were so short, it made your eyes water to look at them. Now they've gone long again – think of Wayne Rooney.'

They all thought of Wayne Rooney for a moment or two in solemn silence.

'Well, Fred, I'll get your jacket,' said Jess, and scuttled back to her bedroom. Fred's grey jacket was lying on her bed. She had set Rasputin the bear to guard it, and he looked reproachfully at her as she picked it up. For an instant she buried her face in it, and breathed in the wonderful, sunshiny and grassy smell of Fred. Anguish flooded through her heart.

She was tempted never to leave her room again, nay, to lock herself in and wrap Fred's jacket round her head for ever, but she simply had to get back downstairs where Ben and Fred and Granny might be having a disastrous and tactless conversation full of misunderstandings. But when she got to the stairs, the hall was empty.

Granny had gone back to the *X-Files*, and the murmur of voices from the kitchen suggested that Ben

169

and Fred had gone in there. As Jess arrived, Fred looked up.

'Ben's just been kind enough to offer me a glass of Coke,' he said, with a hint of hidden outrage. Jess knew how he felt. It should be Fred offering Ben a Coke if anything. The debris of their snack lay all over the table, somehow embarrassing, like scattered underwear.

'However, I'm on a very restricted diet at the moment,' Fred went on. 'Dust and ashes, with just a dash of brackish water from the Pool of Despond. So you must excuse me this time. Gotta go – on the stroke of ten I turn into a tube of fungicide.' He backed away towards the door, kind of nodding and shifting about in his adorable embarrassed Fred kind of way.

'Shame ...' said Ben. *Shut up, Jones, don't say another word*, thought Jess. *Or if you say anything, say you've got to go too.* 'Jess was telling me you, uh, won't be able to be in her show at Christmas because of, urm – *Twelfth Night*.'

'Seems not,' said Fred, pulling a strange face which expressed some kind of pain and regret. 'The rehearsal schedule is a Life Sentence.'

'Well, I'm gonna do what I can – which, let's face it, is, um, like, nothing at all, anyway,' said Ben.

'There you are,' said Fred to Jess with a strange old-fashioned flourish of his arm. 'I told you you'd find somebody to help. Can't wait to see it. The Jones and Jordan Show. It has a certain something. Even alliteration. Certainly beats Jordan and Parsons. That sounds like a firm of crooked lawyers. Well, cheers.' And Fred was gone. The front door slammed – hollowly, or so it seemed to Jess – behind him.

A moment of absolute desolation overwhelmed her for a minute. She was forced to pick up the dirty plates and glasses and wash them, so Ben wouldn't see the despair on her face.

'Fred's so kind of totally, you know, like, brilliant, isn't he?' mused Ben. 'What was all that stuff about – what was it – illustration?'

'Alliteration,' said Jess, wiping down the table with a kind of controlled ferocity. Heartbreak makes the home grow cleaner, that's for sure.

'What's that?' enquired Ben.

'Alliteration – we did it in English. It's when words start with the same letter, like Jones and Jordan.'

'Oh,' said Ben, thinking, and a funny little smile crossed his face for a moment. 'I always, um, you know, hated my name. But it sounds better like that.'

Jess was so desperate for him to leave she was in danger of picking him up bodily and hurling him through the splintering glass of the window. But instead she resorted to massive hints. She yawned and stretched.

'Sorry!' she said. 'I'm totally shattered. It's been a hell of a day.'

'Yeah, yeah, I must go,' said Ben. He gave her an awkward little salute. There was something quite sweet about him despite his limited IQ and ludicrous good looks. At the front door he paused.

'You and Fred – you're, um, uh, back together again, then?' he asked, looking at the floor, then at the door.

'Oh yes,' said Jess. 'We met by chance at the Health Centre and it all got sorted, thanks.'

'Great,' said Ben. 'Great. That is good news. Brilliant.' And he nodded, and went out. He walked straight down the path, and turned to wave from the garden gate. He was lit briefly by a street lamp before being swallowed up by the dark. He looked kind of vulnerable out there for a minute. Jess shivered and went back indoors.

She sat by herself in the kitchen. The light seemed harsh. She saw her face reflected in the glass of the back door. She looked like an old Victorian photograph of someone criminally insane.

How could everything have gone so wrong? If

only Ben hadn't come – but he wouldn't have come if she hadn't borrowed his clothes – and she wouldn't have had to borrow them if she hadn't fled to the school field and thrown herself into the mud.

What must Fred be thinking? Should she send him a text? What did he mean by saying he was living on a diet of dust and ashes? Was it a message about how tormented he was? Was he tormented because of their misunderstanding? Or was it just Fred being Fred?

Her fingers itched to ring him on his mobile, but if it was the answering machine, she wouldn't be able to say a word. And the call records function would eventually inform Fred that he had missed *another* call from her. And if he didn't answer that one either, it could only mean that he did indeed hate her. Passionately.

There was only one thing to do: go to bed. Jess was absolutely shattered. She dragged herself into Granny's room and kissed her goodnight.

'Thanks for coming to the doctor's with me, dear,' Granny said.

Jess patted Granny's head. 'No problem, Granny,' she said. 'I'm glad it's only an ageing neck!'

Jess was just falling asleep when her mobile buzzed. She grabbed it. Was it a text from Fred?

No, it was only Flora.

HAD A FAB EVENING HOPE ALL'S WELL WITH YOU BABE. LU, FLO XXX

It seemed like a message from another planet.

20

SIT NOT ON THE LOO READING CELEB GOSSIP MAGAZINES WHEN THOU SHOULDST BE DOING MATHS HOMEWORK

Jess went to sleep, but in the middle of the night she was woken up by Mum coming upstairs rather noisily. Good Lord! It was 2am! Mum had never been a dirty stop-out in the past. Until recently her idea of a wild night out was staying in the garden weeding the carrots until it was dark. Jess sighed, turned over and plunged back into a dull but unnerving dream about a house with no floor.

'Jess!' Suddenly she was awakened by a distant call. It was Granny's voice. Sunshine was coming in under Jess's curtains. It was 8.15am! Dear God in heaven! Jess shot from the bed instantly and ran out on to the landing. 'Are you awake, Jess?' Granny was calling from the bottom of the stairs. 'I think your mum must have overslept!'

'OK, Granny, thanks!' said Jess. 'I'll wake her up!'

Eight fifteen. This was a total disaster. No way could she get to school on time. She was going to be late – again. Then she suddenly realised Mum still hadn't written the letter explaining why Jess had missed a morning's school, the day she had pretended to be sick in order to do the homework she'd forgotten to do the night before. It seemed impossible to lead an ordinary life without getting entangled in endless melodramas. Jess ran into her mum's bedroom.

'Mum! Mum!' she called. 'Get up! It's a quarter past eight! You didn't wake me and now I'm going to be late again! Get up and write a letter to Miss Thorn saying I was ill on Tuesday!'

Only a groan came from the bed. The bedclothes moved feebly. Jess's heart sank. She recognised the telltale signs of a major migraine.

'Sorry, darling,' croaked Mum. 'I've got a terrible headache. Can you ring the library and tell them I won't be in today?'

'I'm not even dressed yet and I'm going to be as late as hell!' said Jess in desperation. 'I'll ask Granny to do it!'

In fact, Granny could write the letter *and* call the library. Mum was in no state even to hold a pen. Jess charged downstairs and ran into Granny's room. Granny was sitting at her little table eating porridge.

'Mum's got a migraine,' said Jess. 'Please could you ring the library and tell them she won't be coming in today?'

'Of course, dear,' said Granny. 'I won't ring them till about ten to nine, though, because they won't be there yet.'

'And another thing, Granny,' said Jess. 'Please could you write a note to my teacher Miss Thorn at school? You remember I was away on Tuesday morning because I was sick?'

'Of course, dear,' said Granny, but she just went on serenely eating her porridge.

'I'm sorry, but please could you do it, like, NOW?' asked Jess. 'I'll get some paper.' She ran up to her mum's study and grabbed a piece of their headed notepaper, and one of Mum's special pens. A faint groan came from Mum's bedroom.

'Jess ... Jess ... Could you bring me a glass of water before you go, darling? In fact, a whole jug of water if possible... No, lemon squash.'

Jess ground her teeth with rage. How could Mum be so irresponsible as to stay out till two o'clock in the morning? No wonder she had a headache. Just who was the parent here, and who the teenager? Jess ran downstairs again. It must be twenty past eight by now and she was still in her pyjamas.

For a horrible moment she had a hallucination that she was running to school in her pyjamas because she didn't have time to get dressed. It was like a ghastly dream. But on the other hand, it was also like what had happened in the real world, just yesterday.

She put the pen and paper in front of Granny. 'Please, Granny,' she said. 'I just have to have a letter from a responsible grown-up, saying why I was away from school on Tuesday.'

Granny put down her spoon and pushed her porridge to one side for a moment.

'Tuesday,' she said, and unfortunately spat a little bit of porridge out on to the paper. 'Oh, sorry, dear,' she said, wiping it off with her hankie. 'How disgusting.' Where she had wiped it, there was a greasy porridgy smear. 'Oh dear,' said Granny, wiping it again. 'What a mess.'

'Leave it!' said Jess, suppressing the urge to scream aloud. 'I'll get another piece!' She ran upstairs and grabbed another piece of paper.

'I'd also like some fruit, please, darling!' called her

mum feebly from her darkened room.

'In a minute! We're just trying to write my note for school!' roared Jess. She was certainly never going to go into nursing. Even if their uniforms were redesigned in a tasteful pink 'n' black.

'Right, Granny,' said Jess. 'Write!'

Granny looked round feebly. 'Oh dear,' she sighed. 'Where are my glasses?' Jess spied them on Granny's sofa table, snatched them and handed them over. Granny put them on, fiddling with her hair. It seemed to take about a day and a half. Then she picked up the pen.

'I must try not to spit on it again!' she grinned. She seemed to think all this was a delightful lark. 'Now,' said Granny, 'what's the date?' Jess had to run to the kitchen to look it up on the calendar. 'Goodness!' said Granny thoughtfully. 'It's my old Aunt Edith's birthday. Still, she won't be expecting a card. She snuffed it in 1978! Ha ha!'

'Please, Granny, can we hurry up?' begged Jess. 'I'm really late for school and I'm not even dressed yet. Now, can you write it by yourself? It's to Miss Thorn. It's to say I was absent on Tuesday morning because I was sick – oh, and you'd better mention that I was absent yesterday because I fell over and got mud on my skirt, and when I came home, you had

179

chest pains and we took you to the doctor. It's not quite true but it is true in parts. Make it up if you like but make it authentic, OK?'

Granny nodded and gave the thumbs up. She started to write. Jess sighed with relief, and ran into the kitchen, where she collected a jug of lemon squash and put some fruit on a plate for Mum.

'Oh, and Granny,' she called, on her way back upstairs, 'can you also say that I was late today because Mum woke up with a migraine and I had to do stuff for her before I left?'

'Of course, dear,' said Granny. 'Leave it to me. I'm not an imbecile.'

Jess certainly hoped not. She placed Mum's fruit and squash on her bedside table, though it was hard to see, in the dark. Mum grabbed her hand. She felt hot and sweaty, but she was shivering.

'I'm so sorry, darling,' said Mum. 'I love you! I'm so sorry I'm such a useless mother ... Could you get me a wet flannel for my head, please? And have you rung the library yet?'

'No!' said Jess. 'Granny's going to do it at ten to nine! There won't be anybody there yet!' She raced out to the bathroom and put a face cloth under the cold tap for a moment. Then she wrung it out and took it in to her mum. The bedside clock said

180

8.30am. Jess almost burst into tears. She was going to be later than anyone has ever been for anything. Irritable Powell would shout so loud the lid of the school would blow off.

'This is too wet, darling,' croaked Mum. 'Can you wring it out a bit more?' Jess grabbed the flannel in exasperation and wrung it out on the floor. 'Jess!' complained Mum. 'Not on the carpet!'

'It's only a few drops of water!' yelled Jess.

'Don't shout! Don't shout!' pleaded Mum.

'OK, sorry, Mum, now I have to get dressed – I'm already going to be half an hour late!'

She raced out, pulled her clothes on and collected an envelope from the study before thundering downstairs.

'I've finished it, love,' said Granny, looking up proudly. 'It's not quite gospel truth, though – I've told a few little white lies as you suggested.'

'That's fine, Granny, that's great!' Jess grabbed the letter and folded it.

'Now,' said Granny, getting up, 'what can I get you for breakfast? Bacon and eggs?'

'No time for breakfast!' said Jess. 'I'm as late as a pig in a war! I've gotta go now, Granny, thanks! And don't forget to ring the library!'

Jess grabbed her schoolbag from the kitchen and

181

ran like hell. Halfway to school she got a stitch and had to slow down to a walk. At this point she wondered if maybe she should read Granny's letter just to make sure it was OK. She read it as she walked along, tripping on paving stones and bumping into lamp posts as she went.

Dear Miss Throne, it said. Miss Throne! What a catastrophic start. *I hope you are well. I expect it's quite an effort getting back to work after the long holidays. I'm sorry Jess was away from school yesterday (this is her grandmother writing by the way, as her mother is indisposed upstairs in a dark room). And also on Tuesday. Jess was sick through a dodgy chicken sandwich. Meat is such a lottery nowadays, isn't it? And then yesterday she came home from school early because she was having giddy spells. I had to take her to the doctor, but she was all right really.*

Then this morning as I write this Jess is very anxious about being late, but I'm afraid she overslept owing to her mother having a migraine. She was out to all hours last night but she deserves a bit of fun after all her troubles. Jess is a good girl really and I hope she appreciates all the efforts her teachers make.

Yours sincerely,

Vera Collins

Jess was tempted for a moment to run away and start a new life in South America. The only thing that prevented her was lack of money. What would Mr Powell and Miss Thorn make of this pile of horse manure? She would soon find out.

21

SNAP NOT AT THY MUM WHEN SHE SUGGESTETH THY ROOM RESEMBLETH A TIP

Jess arrived panting at Mr Powell's door, tried to get her breath back and compose herself, and knocked.

'Come in!' shouted Mr Powell. Even his *Come ins* were louder than other people's. Jess opened the door, her legs shaking with fright. Mr Powell looked up from behind his desk. Jess stepped inside and closed the door behind her – though she knew that once he began to shout, mere timber would be no protection for the outside world. Such a marvellous concept, the outside world. Would she ever manage to regain it, or would she die right here on the carpet?

'I'm very sorry I'm late,' said Jess, handing over the letter. 'We've had a really difficult time at home recently.'

'So how is your grandmother?' asked Irritable Powell, opening the envelope.

Jess was startled. Then she remembered the last time she had spoken to Mr Powell, he thought Granny was suffering a major cardiac crisis. Oh hell! Granny hadn't mentioned the heart attack scare at all – had instead invented some preposterous line about Jess feeling giddy. Jess herself would never lie again. Absolute truth was her only hope. She would throw herself on Mr Powell's mercy.

'She's fine, thank you, sir,' said Jess. 'It was just a heart scare, um – I think it was indigestion, really.' This didn't count as a new lie – it was just the old one, reheated. Jess would start telling the truth immediately, from now on, sure, but she wasn't sure she was ready to confess to old lies just yet.

Mr Powell's eyes ran swiftly over the letter. He frowned slightly. Oh God! How soon after the first frown would the shouting start? He looked up. His eyes were like lasers.

'What's this about you staying out to all hours?' he asked, looking severe.

'That's not me, that's my mum,' said Jess. Thank God that for once it was her mum who had been naughty! It was so wonderful, telling the truth. It felt kind of fresh and safe and shiny. She would always tell the truth from now on. Always.

'My mum's had to take on extra work in the evenings. She teaches English to Japanese people.' It wasn't really a lie to expand Nori into a whole Oriental gang. It made Mum's job sound even more stressful. 'She had to go out with them last night – to some kind of meeting – and she didn't get back till two.'

'Your grandmother doesn't mention the heart scare at all,' said Mr Powell, frowning even more ferociously. Jess's whole body started to tremble.

'The trouble is, you see …' she said, and her voice dropped almost to a whisper.

'What?' asked Mr Powell, looking majorly harsh. What could she possibly say that would touch his heart and completely disarm him? She so longed for him to smile at her and offer her sweets. Or failing that, just to stop frowning and interrogating. Suddenly an idea occurred to Jess, like a bright red apple hanging in the air between them. She reached for it.

'The trouble is …' she went on, 'my granny's, well, she's suffering from dementia. Just slightly. Just a bit. I don't know whether she actually did have those heart pains yesterday. But the thing is, today she's got no memory of them at all. That's why her letter's a bit – you know. Odd.'

Mr Powell's face changed. The frown faded.

Instead he looked concerned. He got up and walked to the window.

'Sit down,' he said. *Bingo!* OK, it was a lie, and a particularly tasteless one, but because Jess was determined to be good from now on, she hoped God would understand. As the teenage carer of a demented person Jess was apparently entitled to sit down. She collapsed on to the chair, which made a farting noise: fwwwwarp! Jess would just have to save that up and laugh about it later.

'I see,' said Mr Powell. There was a long pause while he looked out of the window. Jess saw a plane fly past behind his head, high up in the sky. She wished she was in it. Mr Powell appeared deep in thought for a moment, then he turned and faced Jess. His face, though deeply serious, was not unkind.

'I have talked with Miss Thorn about the problems you've been having,' he said. 'And we agreed to put you On Report with Loss of Leisure until the end of next week.' He handed her a card with the timetable set out on it.

'Every time you have a lesson, you must get the teacher to sign this card,' said Mr Powell. 'You bring the card to me at the end of school every day. You will report to me first thing every morning at 8.45. You won't go to registration with your class. At mid-morning break you will come straight here and do schoolwork.'

He indicated a desk and chair in the corner of his room. 'You will be allowed fifteen minutes for lunch, and then you will come here and spend the rest of the lunch break here, too – from one o'clock till afternoon school begins. You'll spend your time here doing schoolwork and homework.'

'Yes, sir,' said Jess meekly.

'Right. Go along to first lesson now. I'll make sure Miss Thorn gets this note. And I expect to see you back here at mid-morning break. Five to eleven at the latest, not a moment later.'

'Yes, sir,' said Jess, scrambling to her feet. She stood, waiting to be dismissed.

'At the end of next week, we'll review your case,' said Mr Powell. Jess nodded humbly and looked down at the carpet. It was a beautiful, flawless cream. 'All right,' said Mr Powell. 'Go to your lesson now. What lesson is it?'

'French,' said Jess.

'Right,' said Mr Powell. 'I'll see you at 10.55.'

'Yes, sir,' said Jess. 'Thank you.'

She went out, taking a huge breath of relief. He hadn't shouted! He hadn't yelled! He hadn't been horrid! Maybe he had a headache too. That mega-lie about Granny having dementia had certainly taken the wind out of his sails. Jess just hoped he never met Granny. Though Granny was quite eccentric, so maybe she would give the impression of being slightly mad. Perhaps that was where Jess had got it from.

Jess arrived in the French lesson, muttered a garbled apology in French, and slunk to her seat. Everyone was writing an exercise. Jess started it, but her head was whirling. Fred was only three desks away, his back to her. She gazed at his back for a moment. He was wearing the grey marl jacket. Just think – only yesterday that jacket had been wrapped round her!

By the end of the lesson, Jess hadn't finished, of course, and there was homework as well. She took the card up to the teacher's desk for Madame Sault to sign. Everybody else trooped out to their next lesson. Madame Sault examined the work Jess had done in the lesson, and then told her to finish it off in the lunch-break and bring it to her by the end of the afternoon.

With a saintly smile, Jess assured her she would, and then rushed off to physics. She absolutely mustn't be late for anything over the next two weeks. She didn't even have a spare moment to text Flora, who was in a different science set. And though in the past she had often texted her actually *in* physics, secretly under the bench, this time her mobile would stay switched off and in her pocket. She knew one false move could result in the biggest trouble ever.

She knew that her name would be posted up on the staffroom noticeboard as being On Report with Loss of Leisure. Every teacher would look at her with suspicion and disapproval. Loss of Leisure was familiarly known among the inmates of Ashcroft School as LOL. Typical of teachers not to realise it also stood for Laughing out Loud.

Jess tried really hard in physics, even though it was about How Precautions Can Be Taken to Ensure that Electrostatic Charge Can Be Discharged Safely. The way things were right now, an electric shock was the least of her problems. In fact, it seemed almost an inviting diversion from her treadmill of gloom and duty. Somehow she had to get a glimpse of Fred – just a glimpse – before her appointment of doom with Mr Powell at 10.55 precisely.

22

LET SHE WHO IS WITHOUT SIN THROW THE FIRST BREAD ROLL

However, Jess didn't see Fred at the start of break. She rushed from the science block to Mr Powell's study, pausing only for the fastest pee since the one in the garden with Mr Nishizawa. She knocked on Mr Powell's door. There was no answer. She waited, then knocked again. No answer. What should she do?

Jess decided just to wait. Her head was in a whirl. She absolutely had to convince Mr Powell that she was a reformed character – or, even better, that she had never been really bad in the first place. It was so retarded that this term had got off to such a vile start.

Since she seemed unexpectedly to have a spare moment, she got out her mobile and texted Flora. **GUESS WHAT! I'M ON LOL TILL THE END OF NEXT WEEK. SEE**

YOU TONIGHT? It was going to be hard keeping in touch with everybody. There was no immediate reply, so she put her phone away.

Ferocious footsteps heralded the arrival of Mr Powell. He looked irritated when he saw her, but did not shout.

'Go in, go in!' he said. 'Knock once, knock twice, if there's no answer, go in and start work.'

'Yes sir,' said Jess, creeping to her desk in the corner. She got out her French work. Mr Powell opened his filing cabinet and searched for a document. His office was immaculately tidy. His pens were arranged in strict formation on his desk, and all the books and papers on his desk were in careful piles with their edges aligned.

Mr Powell found his document and sat down, reading it with a slight frown. Jess began her French. Then her phone buzzed in her pocket. Mr Powell looked up with a scowl and an actual growl, and held out his hand.

'Switch the thing off and give it to me,' he said. 'You can hand it in every morning and get it back at the end of school.'

Jess switched it off – not before noticing it was Flora replying to her message. She got up and handed the phone over to Mr Powell. He pulled out a drawer of his desk and put it in there. Jess went back to her work.

Strangely, it was much easier to concentrate in Mr Powell's office. He ignored her and at one stage even went out for a couple of minutes. By the end of break Jess had caught up with the French she had missed that morning by being late. She went off to the next lesson, and spent the rest of the morning in the care-free idyll that was double maths.

Then Jess had fifteen minutes for lunch. Where was Flora? And even more crucial, where was Fred? She raced to the canteen. There was a long queue and a tantalising smell of baked potatoes. But no Flora and no Fred. She went to the tuck shop next door. The two Fs weren't there either, but Jodie was buying some crisps. She wanted to know all about being on LOL and what it was like in Irritable Powell's office.

Jess told her in gory detail, then glanced at her watch. Oh no! She only had two minutes left to get some lunch. She bought a sandwich and a chocolate milk, but there was no time to eat now. She put them in her bag and ran back to Mr Powell's office. She knocked, and this time he answered. She went in, and took her place at the desk. Mr Powell barely looked up.

Jess now started on her French homework. It only took about twenty minutes, and as she finished it, her tummy gave a long, rambling rumble like distant thunder. She was starving! Stealthily she reached down into her bag. The sandwich was smiling up at her from inside its clear plastic wrap. WORRA WORRA WORRA WORRA! roared her stomach at the sight of it.

Very quietly Jess lifted the sandwich out. She would try and peel off the plastic which sealed the packaging without making a noise. Mr Powell was engrossed in adding something up. He was glued to his calculator with an intense frown. Jess lifted the tab of the sandwich wrap and pulled gently.

EEEEEEEEEERUYEEEEARUCH! yelled the plastic. Mr Powell looked up and glared.

'No food and drink in my office!' he snapped.

'Sorry,' said Jess. 'There was such a queue at the –'

'Never mind that,' said Mr Powell. 'Put it on my desk.'

He pulled a tissue out of a box on the side shelf and laid the tissue out on his desk like a tablecloth for a dolls' tea party. Jess got up and placed her sandwich on the tissue, still in its plastic container but now with the side panel gone, so the fabulous smell of bread, cheese and pickle could waft through the room and torture her.

'Anything else?' asked Mr Powell.

'Only a chocolate milk,' replied Jess.

'Out here, please,' he said, tapping the desk with a fatigued sigh as if a chocolate milk was tiresome and irritating, rather than the best drink in the world. Jess fetched it and placed it on the tissue next to the sandwich. Then she went back to her work.

Her tummy rumbled again. Mr Powell got up, put the document back in his filing cabinet, stretched, mussed up his hair, looked out of the window, and then said, 'Right. I'm going to lunch. You just carry on. What are you working on now?'

'Maths, sir,' said Jess. He nodded and went out.

It was really weird being in Mr Powell's room on her own. Just a couple of yards away was his filing cabinet, probably full of the most private stuff about people in school.

Maybe Rory Burnett, a famous stud in the sixth form, had been seduced by Miss Parfitt the gym teacher, Ashcroft School's very own *Baywatch* Babe.

Or maybe the head teacher Mrs Tomkins had secretly given birth to multi-racial twins during the school holidays. Or maybe Mr Powell and Miss Thorn had got a thing going and were planning to elope to Martinique, and all Miss Thorn's love letters to him were hidden away in there, tied up with pink ribbon and liberally doused with Armani's *She*.

Jess shook her head to wipe out these distracting possibilities and plunged back into her maths. The smell of the sandwich came creeping across to torture her. Yet another salvo of tummy rumbles broke out, like distant shelling in the Great War. She was so tempted just to have a bite – or one tiny swig of chocolate milk. But she knew that the first thing Mr Powell would do when he got back was look at her lunch to make sure it hadn't been touched.

She soldiered bravely on. Then another thought occurred to her. Maybe CCTV was set up in this office – so if she gave in to temptation and devoured her food, ransacked his drawers and drew moustaches on the photo of his wife and children, every heroic moment would be captured on priceless footage. She couldn't actually see a CCTV camera, but she'd been caught out that way before, at Tiffany's party.

She closed her eyes tight to wipe out the memory of that awful episode, and then went back to maths. Amazingly Jess finished her maths homework shortly afterwards. She was now up to date, having done all the homework set that day – and it wasn't even the end of lunchtime. The feeling was absolutely glorious.

Being On Report with LOL was certainly a prison sentence, but on the other hand, having finished her homework already was quite a liberation. Even more liberating was the moment when the bell went for afternoon school, when Jess performed a speedy exit from Mr Powell's office and consumed her lunch in three minutes flat on the way to registration. It wasn't much of a lunch, but she would be able to pig out in front of the TV tonight without lying to Mum or experiencing a moment's guilt. Or maybe she'd even be able to establish contact with Fred and sort everything out between them.

The afternoon passed swiftly: English (in which Miss Thorn completely ignored her, which was restful) and double art. Then she went back to Mr Powell's office as instructed. Oh no! He was shouting at somebody in there! She didn't dare knock. She just waited outside in misery.

Eventually the shouting stopped and the door opened. A large boy with ginger hair came out. His face was very red and his eyes were kind of moist. He and Jess confronted each other for an instant, and she knew that whenever she ran into him in school again, they would both think of this moment.

Then she knocked, and Mr Powell called her in. She presented the card, signed by all the teachers who had taught her that day.

'All right,' said Mr Powell. 'See you tomorrow at 8.45 sharp.' He handed over her mobile phone.

'Yes,' said Jess. 'Thank you. Goodbye.' It sounded a bit odd, trying to be polite. Walking on eggshells.

'Goodbye,' said Mr Powell, turning back to some papers and picking up the phone.

Jess went out to the school gates, where a lot of people were getting on buses. She looked around for Flora and Fred.

'Jess!'

She turned. It was Ben Jones and Mackenzie.

'Hey, I told Mackenzie all about your comedy show and he's, like …'

'I'm well up for it,' said Mackenzie.

'Er, just a min – have you seen Flora?' asked Jess.

'Oh, she's gone to the drama studio,' said Mackenzie. 'They're having a readthrough of *Twelfth Night*.' That meant there was no chance of seeing Flora or Fred, either.

'Let's go down the café,' said Mackenzie, 'and make some plans for the show, then, yeah?'

Jess's heart sank. She had a feeling that after the restful day with Mr Powell, things were now going to get quite stressful again. And she was right.

23

WHOSO WALKETH UPRIGHTLY SHALL BE SAVED, BUT YE COUCH POTATOES SHALL BE CAST INTO THE BURNING FIERY FURNACE (AND EMERGE AS OVEN CHIPS)

The Dolphin Café was as cosy and steamy as usual, but somehow being here was already an ordeal.

'Right,' said Mackenzie, rubbing his hands together in an irritating way, as if he was in charge. 'How many sketches have you written so far?'

Jess was offended by his brisk manner. It was *so* not his business. She had written those sketches with Fred.

'Oh, about four or five,' she said. 'But –'

'Yeah, well, if you can let us have some copies of them, that would be great,' said Mackenzie. 'So I can see what we're working with.'

Jess already wanted to kill him, and they'd only

been here for two minutes.

'The thing is,' she said, speaking slowly so as to avoid losing her temper, 'I wrote them with Fred – in fact, Fred wrote most of them.'

'Yeah, yeah, whatever,' said Mackenzie. 'He'll get a credit on the programme, right?'

Jess bit her lip and tried to banish the feeling of being mugged in public. She said nothing and took a sip of her hot chocolate. It was too hot and burned the lip she had so recently bitten. Ben was looking at her with a kind of worried frown. Suddenly, unexpectedly, he spoke.

'Maybe that stuff you wrote with Fred ... maybe you'd want to keep it for later, when you can, like, uh, perform it with him?' said Ben.

Jess gave him a grateful look. 'Well, it does seem a bit tight to use the material without at least asking him,' she said.

'No problem,' said Mackenzie. 'You can ring him tonight, yeah? I'm sure he'll be cool about it.'

Jess didn't want to admit to them that she and Fred were no longer in daily communication, so she shrugged and said OK.

'I've had some brilliant ideas anyway,' said Mackenzie. 'And we'll need lots of new material. We could even revive the band.'

'Flora wouldn't be able to be in it,' said Jess. 'She's

in *Twelfth Night*.'

'Yeah, yeah, I know,' said Mackenzie. 'But you could be the singer instead.'

'Me, sing?' said Jess in dismay. 'You cannot be serious. My voice is a sound that can make babies cry in the womb.'

'Hey, that was funny!' said Mackenzie. 'Write that down!' He turned to Ben, who didn't even have a pen or paper. Ben just shrugged and looked at Jess with an apologetic air. 'Anyway,' Mackenzie went on, 'the worse you sing the better, because it's supposed to be a comedy band anyway, OK?'

'There's no need to explain that to me of all people!' Jess couldn't help snapping. 'It was my idea to make the band a comedy act in the first place.'

'Yeah, yeah, brilliant, I know,' said Mackenzie. He had the hide of a rhino.

'I don't want the band to be in it anyway,' said Jess. 'I'd rather do something new. Something like, *Here's a performance by some folk musicians from Jacuzzistan, where hairdressing is a performance art.* Then you perform a tune on the scissors, hairbrush and comb.'

'Yeah, great idea in principle, I like it,' said Mackenzie, as if he was the Director or something. 'But there's going to be problems with the amplification with a sketch like that. They'd never hear it at all at the back row of the gallery.'

'Well, why stop at making it quiet?' said Jess, trying desperately not to get rattled, but all the same getting rattled. 'Why don't we have a totally silent musical number? Two of us could come on and open our mouths in a kind of synchronised miming, total silence, and the other one could do that sort of signing stuff they do for deaf people.'

'Yeah, yeah, fantastic, great idea,' said Mackenzie, as if he wasn't really listening properly at all. 'Anyway, I was going to tell you about my ideas, yeah?'

'Yeah,' said Jess, politely. 'OK.' He might have some good ideas after all.

'Well, you know Gollum in *The Lord of the Rings*? I think he could be the kind of presenter of the show. *And now, my pwecious sketch about hairdwessing as performance art ...*' Mackenzie did a very bad imitation of Gollum. 'I could kind of scuttle about saying Gollum-like things about all the sketches, yeah?' grinned Mackenzie.

'Hmmmm,' said Jess. How could she tell him politely that this idea was rubbish and his imitation stank? 'Yeah, possibly, but you know, I've always seen you more as a kind of Frodo Baggins. In fact, you do look rather like him.'

Jess had thought this was a compliment, but Mackenzie reacted as if he had been made to eat tortoise poo.

'Frodo Baggins!' he said. 'But he's so like totally boring! All he ever does is look tortured and get dumped on by everybody.'

Jess felt so exasperated she couldn't speak for a moment. Mackenzie pulled his Gollum face again. Any minute now he was going to say something to do with the word 'pwecious' in what he imagined was Gollum's voice. Jess was not sure she could endure any more of it without vomiting.

'I don't think,' Ben said, 'we should do too much, like, of people from films 'n' stuff. I think it's better … if it's, you know, um, original?'

'Quite right!' cried Jess, giving him a radiant smile. 'Tell you what, Mackenzie, why don't we all go away and make a list of ideas for sketches, and meet again to discuss them tomorrow?' She couldn't wait to escape. 'Sorry, but I'm in a major homework crisis and I'm On Report with LOL. So I've got to get organised for a couple of weeks. After which, of course, I can slump into my usual swamp.'

'OK, but e-mail us your scripts, yeah?' said Mackenzie in a bossy way. Jess ignored him. She got up. Ben also got to his feet. He looked right into her eyes, and he seemed in a strange kind of state. He so obviously wanted to apologise for Mackenzie behaving like an idiot.

'Yeah, well, thanks for letting us – be in your show,' he said. 'Hope we can, uh, contribute something – you know.' He shrugged. Jess squeezed his arm. He was the sweetest guy in the world.

'Don't worry, Ben,' she said. 'It's going to be wonderful.' Then she rushed out and raced off towards home. It was, in fact, going to be terrible.

Still, at least the evening stretched ahead of her, gloriously free of homework. She sent Flora a text asking her to ring when she got in. Jess was desperate for a jolly good moan. Flora would also be able to tell her how Fred seemed. Maybe she could even ask Flora to ask Fred … no! That was madness.

Jess barged in through the front door calling, 'Hi Granny, I'm home! It's a jungle out there! Bring me that cooked breakfast you promised me! It's only nine hours late!'

'We're in the sitting room, dear!' called Granny in a strange public sort of voice. Jess waltzed in. And oh, spit in the custard again! Nori was sitting there.

'He's come for his lesson, haven't you, dear?' said Granny. 'Your mum's still in bed so she can't do it but he says he just wants to practise a few things. Would you mind taking him off and going through with it, love? I want to get back to *Emmerdale*.' She said the last bit very fast and quietly, as if she was ashamed of it. As indeed she should be. Granny was a pathetic soap addict.

'Mr Nishizawa!' said Jess. 'How lovely to see you! Come through to the kitchen and we can do your English conversation.'

Mr Nishizawa got up and bowed. Thank God Mackenzie had never met him. If Mackenzie ever made fun of Mr Nishizawa, Jess would personally kill him in a long, slow way involving his nostrils and a handful of uncooked spaghetti.

She adored Mr Nishizawa. He was immensely cool. Although how much more delightful it would have been if Mr Nishizawa had *not* been sitting here requiring attention when she got home.

They went through to the kitchen and Jess put the kettle on and got out the posh biscuits.

'So, in fact –' Mr Nishizawa began, disastrously, to speak, '– wondering an indisposal, parent regret, how far time usual in general so?'

Jess was *so never* going to have a career teaching English as a foreign language. Even if the job came with a free house by the sea and an adorable golden puppy. In fact, ludicrous as it seemed, the way things were panning out, she couldn't wait to get back to the divine serenity of Mr Powell's office.

24

THOU SHALT NOT COVET THY BEST MATE'S BOYFRIEND, YEA EVEN IF HE BE LIKE UNTO A GLAMOROUS FOOTBALLER

Talking to Mr Nishizawa was tiring, and listening to him was even worse. It was physically exhausting, trying to understand him. Jess realised halfway through that every time he spoke, she screwed her face up as if she had toothache. However did Mum bear it night after night? She must be just longing for the hour to pass, secretly watching the clock over Mr Nishizawa's shoulder, as Jess was now. Eventually, however, after about seven years, the lesson came to an end and he went away.

Granny had made a wonderful supper – a kind of cheesy potato pie thing with baked beans, which was Jess's favourite meal in the world. Jess ate a portion the size of France, abandoning all plans to achieve a slim, sexy figure. If Fred didn't love her any more, she would give up on men altogether.

'Your mum's asleep, love – so it's my job to nag you about your homework,' said Granny.

'Aha! Did it all in school, Granny! Got the whole evening free!'

'Really? You're not telling me a little fib are you, dear?'

'No! I swear on the sacred memory of Grandpa with his crazy hats and enormous pixie-like ears!' said Jess. It was really wonderful, having done the homework at school. If only she'd been On Report with Loss of Leisure for the past two years.

Although the Loss of Leisure bit was tough. It was so hard to keep in touch with everybody. When finally at 8.30 Flora rang, Jess seized the phone so desperately she almost swallowed it.

'Hi Jess! How are you, babe? How's it going? Is it grim being On Report?'

'Oh no, Mr Powell's quite a pussycat really. We're practically dating. How was the readthrough?'

'God, it was so awful! I got so many words wrong. Still, so did Jodie. She's playing Olivia. I wish you'd auditioned for it, babe – you'd have been heaps better than her.'

'Thanks, but I wouldn't want to spend any more time with Thorn than absolutely necessary.'

'She's not so bad when she's directing plays,' said Flora. 'She's still kind of on edge, but she's not so weird and harsh. But hey – listen! Jack Stevens is so absolutely gorgeous! He sat next to me in the readthrough and then he walked home with us afterwards! Guess who he reminds me of?'

'Er – let me see, he's kind of dark and charismatic, right?'

'Right!'

'Hitler?'

'Don't be an idiot, Jess! No, he reminds me of Mark Darcy in *Bridget Jones*, only younger of course.'

'Sounds OK for starters,' said Jess, desperately wanting to turn the conversation around to Fred, but realising that she would have to let Flora rave on about Jack Stevens for a little bit first. After Flora had described in detail Jack's long dark eyelashes, beautiful square hands and strange smouldering Darcyish scowl, Jess finally thought it was time for her own agenda.

'And how was Fred?' she asked.

'Oh, he was so funny! We all cracked up. He even made Miss Thorn laugh. I think she's got a bit of a thing about Fred. You should watch out!'

'My English Teacher Stole My Boyfriend territory, eh?' said Jess. 'Well, I'll make a fortune selling my story to the papers. But, er … did Fred say anything afterwards?'

'What, to me, you mean? No, he was talking to Jodie. They were messing around. Malvolio's Olivia's steward, of course, so she was giving Fred orders on the way home afterwards and he was pretending to crawl and drool over the hem of her garment, and stuff.'

Jess felt sick. She would kill both Fred and Jodie tomorrow, with the nearest heavy object. Although after all that cheese pie, she *was* the nearest heavy object. Right. She would fall on them both. For a moment she could say nothing – the sour feeling inside made it impossible.

'What's wrong, babe? You and Fred are OK again, aren't you?'

'Well, no, if you really want to know,' said Jess. 'We're not. We met at the Health Centre yesterday sort of by accident, and he lent me his jacket, but when he came round to my house afterwards to collect it, Ben was here.'

'That Ben! Always sniffing around you! If only you still fancied him, you two could become an item.'

'Oh no,' said Jess, 'Ben doesn't fancy me even

remotely. He told me last term he didn't want a girl-friend at all, and anyway, I couldn't be happy with him for ten seconds now I know what it's like being with Fred.'

'Sorry, Jess, I've got to go,' said Flora abruptly. 'My dad's started to do homework mimes at me. Don't panic about it, OK? Play a waiting game. We'll go out on Saturday and give you a makeover. Then we'll have a picnic on Sunday and invite Fred along. He'll soon come to heel, don't worry.'

Jess put the phone down feeling a bit more cheerful. It would be nice to have a makeover on Saturday, and the Sunday picnic was a terrific idea. She and Fred had shared so many fantastic picnics in the park during the summer. Surely they would manage to sort out their misunderstanding just as soon as they got some time together?

But when would that be? Maybe there would be too many other people around at the weekend. Jess was so tempted to ring Fred right now. She had to remove herself physically from the phone to avoid grabbing it. She went upstairs and as she'd already done her homework, she decided to abandon the habits of a lifetime and tidy her room.

When it was all done she even combed Rasputin's fur, which made him look somehow rather like Oscar

Wilde. Still it was only 9.30. Not too late to ring. She went into the next room, which was Mum's study, and picked up the phone. Her fingers shook. She dialled Fred's home number. Moments later, Fred's dad answered in a gruff, bad-tempered voice that suggested that in Fred's house it was already 3am.

'Sorry,' said Jess, bottling out. 'Wrong number.'

'Jess!' called her mum feebly from her bedroom. 'Who are you ringing, darling?'

Jess went into her mum's room. She was sitting up in bed looking a lot better and drinking a glass of water.

'Oh, I just rang Flora because there was something I forgot to tell her earlier,' said Jess. 'But I got the wrong number and then I thought maybe it's rather late.' More lies already. She hoped God wouldn't notice.

Her mum smiled and nodded, and then patted the bed. Jess sat down. Her mum clasped her hand.

'I'm glad you're feeling better, Mum,' said Jess. 'You've stopped looking like a Martian.'

'Yes,' said Mum. She smiled and squeezed Jess's hand. Then she started to look kind of strange. 'I'm a bit overtired, that's all,' she went on. 'In fact, I'm going to have a little break this coming weekend. I'm going to Brighton.'

'Fantastic!' said Jess. 'Can I come?'

'Well …' Her mum hesitated. 'I'm going to see an old school friend. It's a bit awkward, really. I don't think she'll have room for the two of us.'

'Oh, I don't care where I sleep!' said Jess. 'I'll sleep on the sofa, the floor, no problem.'

'Well …' Mum let go of Jess's hand and started to fiddle with the bedcover. 'It's not going to be much fun, because her husband's just left her and she wants to talk.'

'I don't mind!' said Jess. 'I'll go out while you're having your heart-to-hearts. I can have the best time. Brighton! It's the coolest place in the world.'

'Yes, but …' Mum hesitated again. 'She doesn't live down near the seafront, she lives several miles inland. And to be honest, darling,' she blushed, 'I need you to stay here and keep an eye on Granny. I'm sorry.'

'Granny's fine on her own!' said Jess. 'She's totally independent. We can get loads of food in for her. She can have her friend round from the bridge club.'

'No, love,' said Mum. 'I'm really sorry, but it isn't going to work, you coming. Not this time. Next time maybe.'

Jess got up off the bed feeling very annoyed.

'In case you hadn't realised, Granny will be even older by next time,' she observed sharply. 'Oh well. Never mind. I expect we'll have a fun weekend going through the photo albums.'

She went out and gave the bedroom door just a little slam. Her mum *had* just had a migraine, but on the other hand, she *was* being intensely irritating.

In bed that night, Jess comforted herself with the thought that it might be better if her mum didn't take her to Brighton for the weekend. There was the chance that if she stayed at home, she and Fred would get together again. Fred could be so sulky and weird when they had misunderstandings. Jess had become totally convinced that it was her job to make the first move. She would transform herself this weekend into a voluptuous diva, and Fred would fall at her feet.

25

SIX DAYS SHALT THOU WORK, BUT ON THE SEVENTH SHALT THOU WATCH WEEPY OLD MOVIES ON TV

Next day was Friday. Jess arrived in good time to walk to school with Flora, who was excited at the prospect of seeing Jack Stevens again. Jess listened patiently to her raptures.

'We've got loads of scenes together, but I know he doesn't fancy me. That girl with red hair was with him at break again yesterday. She's my understudy, so she has to be at all our rehearsals too. It's so tight!'

'She hasn't got a chance,' said Jess. 'Don't forget you are the most beautiful girl since Helen of Troy.'

'Oh, so I'm not as good-looking as Helen of Troy, huh?' laughed Flora. 'Fine friend you turned out to be.'

They had a great time walking to school, so Jess

did not mention her tragic heartbroken state vis-à-vis Fred. She knew it would destroy the atmosphere. It was lovely seeing Flora being happy and excited. If only she had auditioned for *Twelfth Night* herself. Then she could be having a ball with Flora and Fred instead of coming close to homicide with Mackenzie and Ben.

She arrived at Mr Powell's office exactly on time, handed over her mobile phone, and went through her morning lessons in a virtuous manner. Indeed, her behaviour would not have disgraced the Virgin Mary when she was at Nazareth High. Last lesson in the morning was French, and Jess even wasted five minutes of her fifteen-minute lunch break helping Madame Sault to carry a box of French books back to the staffroom. She hoped God was watching.

However, now she had barely seven minutes left for lunch. She was checking her watch on her way to the tuckshop when she rounded a corner and bumped into somebody. It was Fred.

He looked startled and blushed bright red. Jess didn't know whether to be encouraged or upset by this. At least it showed he had an emotional reaction when he saw her. But maybe it was horror and embarrassment. After a few moments of frozen awkwardness Fred managed to switch into comedy mode.

He executed a low bow.

'We must stop meeting like this,' he said.

'Tiresome, isn't it?' said Jess, her heart beating madly. 'One would so much rather be having one's fingernails pulled out by Spanish torturers.'

'Indeed,' said Fred. 'Or possibly being forced to eat live worms like a celebrity in the jungle.'

'Speaking of eating worms,' said Jess, following a mad impulse, 'are you doing anything on Sunday? Flora and I are planning a picnic in the park. Wanna come?' It might just be the moment she had been waiting for. It might be the way back to paradise. Not to talk about their misunderstanding, but just to take a leap in the dark and start again.

But Fred's body language was not encouraging. He winced. He cocked his head to one side. He shrugged.

'Alas,' he said. 'My parents have got this trip planned. We're going to see my uncle in Yorkshire. He lives in a freezing old farmhouse with three incontinent sheepdogs, so you can imagine how much I'm looking forward to going.'

'You lucky thing! One would kill for such a weekend,' said Jess, trying to look completely relaxed about the whole thing. The awful truth was, she would indeed kill for such a weekend. If only she could spend the weekend with Fred, she would gladly endure being peed on and pooed on by the whole animal kingdom. Even elephants.

'Well …' she managed to gather herself into some kind of order, 'I've got to go. I've got a hot date with Mr Powell in the throbbing privacy of his office.'

'Delightful prospect!' said Fred. 'You're such a party animal. I, alas, will spend the lunch break being spat on by Jodie. Rehearsing, you know.'

And he gave a strange, ducking little nod and turned away. Jess could hardly contain her tears. How dare Jodie spit on him! That was *her* job. This *Twelfth Night* business was a total nightmare. If only Shakespeare had sprained his wrist that week and, instead of writing a play, pigged out on marzipan in front of the TV. No, wait, they didn't have TV in those days. Well, he could have pigged out in a tavern somewhere. Never trust bald guys. They always feel they have something to prove.

She felt intensely irritated at the thought of Jodie and Fred within spitting distance of each other. But beyond that was a deeper gloom about the impossibility of seeing Fred this weekend. The picnic didn't seem like such a good idea now. She would rather spend Sunday reading the Bible, eating gruel and listening to Granny reminisce about Great Blisters of the Past than attend a Fredless picnic.

She behaved with spotless virtue for the rest of the day. Mr Powell even said 'Have a good weekend', when he dismissed her after school. He handed her mobile phone over. 'I daresay your life will be in ruins without this,' he observed.

'My life is in ruins anyway,' said Jess. It was quite a good moment, somehow.

Next day Flora came round. Mum had left for Brighton the night before and Granny had gone off to play cards with some fabulous old dears called Jenny, Irene and Deirdre. Jess had the house to herself. But she didn't feel very festive when she let Flora in.

'I haven't got any money for a makeover,' she said. 'I haven't got the motivation either.'

'Never mind,' said Flora. 'I've got a new camera – look!'

Good God! It was a state-of-the-art digital camera. Flora said her mum had given it to her just for getting into *Twelfth Night*. How the other half lived! Still, at least Jess had a rich best friend. Maybe in their future lives she could become Flora's vivacious but vulgar maidservant. In fact, why wait till the future? That was practically the situation already.

'I've had this fantastic idea,' said Flora. 'I want to

do some photos which are a sort of parody of Great Masters. You know – like The Scream.' She performed a perfect mime of the famous Munch painting. 'And you could give it a caption, like, *Oh no! I left my tennis racquet on the bus!*'

'It might be better without captions at all,' said Jess. 'We could make it a visual gag, you know. Like you could do the scream, but with an ice cream on your head.'

'*I scream for ice cream,*' said Flora. 'Yessss!'

They went up to Jess's mum's bedroom, and ransacked her extensive wardrobe of dated clothing.

'Mum can never bear to throw anything away,' said Jess. 'Hey! Guess the painting!' She chose a blue scarf and wound it round her head, then searched through her mum's jewellery box for a pearl earring. It was a clip-on, so she clipped it on to her nostril instead and then turned and looked at Flora over her shoulder.

'*Girl with a Pearl Nose-ring!*' laughed Flora, and took a photo. 'Next?'

'Well, as you so famously resemble the goddess Venus, it's got to be Botticelli!' said Jess. 'No need to take your clothes off. Just do The Birth of Venus, you know. If only Mum had a blonde wig a yard long. But I'm afraid for that kind of thing we'd have to visit Dad, who let's face it, is three hundred miles away.

Never mind – hold your hands over your rude bits and look as if you're burping!' Jess took a photo. 'The Burp of Venus!' she said. 'OK, that one has a caption. I admit it – words are useful sometimes.'

After that Jess did a Mona Lisa with her teeth blacked out (the old jokes are sometimes the best) and then they made up Flora to look like Marilyn Monroe, with a big pout just like the Andy Warhol print, only with a can of soup on her head.

'A brilliant marriage of Warhol's two best known twentieth century icons!' said Jess in a posh art historian's voice. Then they fed the images into Jess's mum's computer and sent them to all their friends.

'Shall we send one to Fred?' asked Flora.

'I don't know …' Jess hesitated. 'I just don't know, right now. He's so weird at the moment. I haven't the faintest idea what he's thinking.'

'That's OK!' said Flora. 'It's a mystery. What is love without periods of misunderstanding and suffering?'

'A hell of a lot better, if you really want to know,' said Jess.

Eventually Granny came back, and Flora had to go home, and the weekend sort of unravelled into an ordinary Saturday night in – though Granny and Jess did celebrate their solitude by getting an Indian takeaway.

'While the cat's away, the mice will play,' said Granny with a wink.

'While the mouse is away, the cats will play, you mean,' said Jess. 'No way could Mum ever be described as a cat.'

On Sunday, Jess watched *Brief Encounter*, a heart-wrenching old film that made her cry a lot, and then, right at the very end, the final moment was disturbed by the doorbell.

'Goddammit!' cried Jess, heading for the hall. She silently cursed whoever it was, knowing for sure Fred would not be back from Yorkshire yet. Although even if he was back from Yorkshire, would he have come round to see her? Would he ever come round again?

She opened the door. There stood Mackenzie, looking important, and Ben Jones, looking kind of furtive and anxious.

'We've had lots of brilliant ideas!' said Mackenzie. 'Can we come in and talk?'

Jess could hardly say no. They came in and sat in the kitchen. Mackenzie described, in blood-curdling detail, how fantastic it would be if he presented the show in the style of Homer Simpson. After two hours of Mackenzie doing bad imitations of Homer, Jess went into automatic pilot. She no longer heard or saw him.

She was reminded of Flora's words yesterday: 'What is love without misunderstanding and suffering?' True, such a life really sucked. But what was suffering and misunderstanding without love? Even worse. How was she going to break the awful news to Mac and Ben that their ideas were atrocious? But even more urgent, how was she going to get them *out of the house right now*? In the end she had to resort to a false report of period pain. Nothing gets rid of guys faster. They simply flee.

26

WORSHIP NOT ARMANI NOR VERSACE FOR THEY ARE FALSE GODS AND BESIDES, I'M NOT MADE OF MONEY

On Monday morning Jess met Fred by accident at the school gate. He was with Tom and Buster.

'How was Yorkshire?' she said. 'I hope you were urinated on by all three sheepdogs.'

'Oh yes,' said Fred. 'And how was your weekend? I hope you were urinated on by a team of Chinese acrobats?'

'Oh, I've moved on from that kind of scene,' said Jess. 'I'm destined for higher things. I'm going to Downing Street next weekend to be crapped on by the Prime Minister.'

The bell rang. Jess ran off to Mr Powell's office, which was, as usual, divinely peaceful. Everything so tidy, so immaculate, so clean. Only Mr Powell's rather wildly curly hair seemed a tad disobedient. Jess wondered if he ever shouted at his own hair. On the other hand, she had often shouted at hers. So perhaps it was the human condition. Maybe if Shakespeare had had more hair to shout at he wouldn't have written so many goddam plays.

Jess handed over her mobile phone as usual, and received a blank card for the signatures of every teacher after every lesson.

'At the end of this week,' said Mr Powell, 'I shall ask for a report on your conduct from all of your teachers. If it's satisfactory, you'll stop being On Report and I hope that when we meet in future, it will be in happier circumstances.'

'Yes, sir,' said Jess. She was determined to be good. Being On Report really sucked. OK, so she finished her homework way before time – something Jess had never experienced before. It was rather pleasant. But Loss of Leisure and having her phone confiscated was a real pain. Flora had rehearsals and music lessons after school. And when Fred was not rehearsing he just seemed to disappear.

Jess did not dare to ring him at the moment. She decided she would wait until the weekend. If Fred said or did something upsetting, she would not trust herself. She might lose it big time and commit some awful new crime, and be back to square one with Mr Powell. And next time he would be sure to shout.

She also used being On Report to postpone any further meetings with Mackenzie and Ben. She promised them she would be back in action the following week, and they would really get stuck into the comedy show then. The thought depressed her terribly, and was a kind of sickening undertone to the whole week.

However, the first four days of the week went by OK. Thursday night always felt kind of promising, because there was only one more day left before Saturday. Jess had finished her schoolwork, and Granny was out playing cards again, so while Mum gave Mr Nishizawa his lesson, Jess watched an old video of *The Rocky Horror Picture Show*.

Eventually she heard her mum seeing Mr Nishizawa out, and then Mum came in and sat down beside her.

'Turn that down for a minute, Jess.'

'But Mum! This is my favourite bit!'

'Just turn it down.'

Jess hit the mute button, feeling rather aggravated. 'What?'

'There's something I've got to tell you.' Jess felt a

sudden qualm of fear.

'What? Is somebody ill? Is Dad OK?'

'No, nobody's ill,' said Mum. 'It's just that, well – I'm going to go away again this weekend.'

'Oh, OK,' said Jess, still watching the TV, where Frank N Furter was strutting about in his basque and ferocious make-up. Jess wondered if she could do a Frank N Furter impersonation in the Christmas Show. Would it work? Double drag? A girl imitating a man in women's clothes?

'I'm going to the Peak District,' said Mum.

'Fine,' said Jess, wondering where she could get a basque like that. Maybe they had some in the costume hire place just behind the bus station.

'With Nori,' said Mum.

Suddenly Jess's obsession with pervy underwear evaporated.

'What? What are you going with him for?' Her mum hesitated, and looked at the carpet. 'Mum!' cried Jess in sudden horror. 'You're not *going out with him*, are you?'

'Well,' said Mum, 'that's really what I'm trying to tell you. Yes.'

'You're having an affair? With *Mr Nishizawa*?'

'It's not an *affair*,' said Mum. 'It's more of a relationship. It's mostly meditating. It's very spiritual.

226

Anyway, why shouldn't I have a relationship with Nori?' She suddenly sounded rather like a rebellious teenager.

'But he's totally unsuitable!' yelled Jess, sounding rather like a disapproving Victorian parent.

'Why?' said Mum. 'You said yourself you thought he was cool. And sweet.'

'Yes, but Mum, he's way younger than you!'

'Only fourteen years younger,' said Mum. 'You wouldn't bat an eyelid if Dad had a boyfriend who was fifteen years younger than him.'

'Yes, but Mum! When you were my age, he was – he was two years old, for God's sake. You would have been, like, his babysitter.'

'Don't be silly, Jess. This is now. Anyway, I've told you all you need to know. I'll be away in the Peak District next weekend. I'm sorry, but these things happen. I thought you'd be happy for me. I've hardly had a date since Daddy and I split up. I've been living the life of a nun.'

'I don't want you to have dates!' yelled Jess. She knew she was being really childish but she couldn't help it. 'Go back to being a nun! Oh my God! Last weekend, when you went to Brighton – you were with him, weren't you?'

'Yes,' said Mum. 'I'm sorry I had to lie to you, but

I wasn't ready to tell you then.'

'Does Granny know?' demanded Jess.

'Not yet. I'll tell her tonight. She'll be pleased for me.'

Jess wasn't so sure.

'Isn't he going back to Japan soon?'

'Yes – in mid-October.'

'So then what?'

Her mum shrugged. It was a ghastly sight, somehow. Jess got up, full of rage and guilt. She went upstairs and slammed her bedroom door behind her. The thought of her mum and Mr Nishizawa, well … getting it on, was too awful for words. But she had to control herself. She just mustn't lose it. She had to stay calm and not go crazy. There was only one more day of being On Report. Then she could explode.

There was a bit of an atmosphere at breakfast on Friday. Granny looked slightly pale. Mum must have told her. But of course nobody was going to mention it.

'Would you like some scrambled egg, Jess?' asked Mum with a strange friendly smile which was somehow not genuine, like a mum in a TV advert.

'No thanks,' said Jess. 'I'm not hungry. I'll get something later.' She kissed Granny and left the house.

She wasn't going to kiss Mum again for some time.

Mum was getting enough kisses anyway, from other sources. At least Granny would never drop that kind of bombshell. *You know my friend Deirdre, Jess – the one I play cards with? Well, I've got to confess, dear – I've fallen passionately in love with her. I was a lesbian all along, and I never guessed! Fancy! I wonder what Grandpa would have said? Anyway, Deirdre and I are off for a weekend in Barcelona. We'll send you a postcard.*

Jess saw Fred briefly in the corridor on her way to Mr Powell's room at break. He was with Tom again. He paused.

'How's things then?' he said. 'Dare one hope that your life is endless torture?'

'It certainly is,' replied Jess. 'I've just discovered that my mum is having a torrid affair with a Japanese schoolboy, and my granny's just come out as an elderly lesbian. Still, these things are sent to provide plots for novels. Gotta go – Mr Powell will be waiting with the electrodes.'

'Shocking!' said Fred, and they parted. Jess wasn't sure which was worse – meeting him alone, or meeting him when he was with somebody. Their comic banter, which used to be so much flirtatious fun, now felt like poisoned arrows.

She arrived at Mr Powell's office and went in. He was on the phone, but he nodded to her, received her mobile and put it in his drawer.

'Good, good!' he said, sounding rather frantic. But not bad-tempered. Jess sat down at her desk and got out her French vocabulary book. She had to learn some words for a test. 'Tell her I'll be there as soon as I can,' said Mr Powell again. 'Just as soon as I've sorted it out with Sheila. Bye!' He rang off, stood up and pulled on his jacket.

'I'm going to be away this lunchtime,' he said to Jess, in a whole different tone of voice: stern and horrid. 'But I want you to come here as usual and do your work. I'll see you at the end of afternoon school if I'm back in time – otherwise, first thing Monday morning. Then I hope we can wind up what has been a distressing episode.'

Jess nodded dumbly. If Mr Powell thought just having to sit in his office all the time was a distressing episode, he was mistaken. Why, it had been the high point of her week. Being alienated from Fred, finding out that her mum was making a fool of herself with a toyboy, having her comedy show hijacked by that bigheaded talentless prat, Mackenzie, that was distressing. Compared with the rest of her life, being On Report was a walk in the park.

The day unrolled. By lunchtime, Jess was absolutely starving. She ran straight to the tuck shop.

There was a queue, of course. You had to queue in a corridor overlooking the school field. Suddenly her heart lurched. Fred and Jodie were down there! Fred was kind of swaggering around Jodie, kissing his hand and bowing. Then – o vile moment! – he moved in on her, took Jodie's hand in his and kissed it, and then kind of rubbed it up against his face.

Jess was almost sick on the spot. In fact, she probably would have been sick if she'd had anything at all to eat recently. She could quite happily have killed Fred, Jodie, and indeed Shakespeare – if he hadn't been already dead. She knew they were only rehearsing – but wait! *Were* they? And why the need for all these extra, private rehearsals on the school field at lunchtime? Weren't the scheduled rehearsals enough?

Jess realised with another sickening lurch that if Fred got interested in another girl, Jodie would be just the type he'd go for. She wasn't particularly pretty, in fact she was quite spotty most of the time, but she was lively, funny and glamorously temperamental.

'Yes?' The girl serving in the tuckshop asked Jess for her order. Jess was suddenly confronted with the idea of food. Although deeply sickened by what she had just seen, she knew she badly needed something to eat. She felt weak and her legs had gone shaky.

'Oh – a pasta salad and a chocolate milk, please,' she said.

'Hi babe!' Flora had appeared. Never had her appearance been more welcome. 'What's the matter?' She looked shocked at Jess's expression.

'God, where to begin?' said Jess, paying for the food and putting it in her bag. 'My life is in total, total ruins.'

'Tell me! What's wrong, babe?' Flora put her arm around her. But Jess caught sight of her watch.

'I can't stop – I've got to go. I mustn't be late for Mr Powell! It's my last LOL! See you after school?'

'Oh – I've got a runthrough then,' said Flora. 'Talk to you tonight, maybe?'

'I'll call you!' said Jess, running off. On the way she remembered that Mr Powell wasn't actually going to be there this lunchtime. She was so tempted to go back, grab Flora, and tell her all her troubles.

But she had a funny kind of feeling that this last LOL was a kind of test. Maybe Mr Powell had installed CCTV to find out if she would turn up and do her schoolwork properly even if he wasn't there. Well, she was going to deliver. She wasn't going to spoil it all at the last minute.

She knocked – even though she knew he wasn't

there – and went in. She sat down at her desk and got out her biology project. She reached for her pen. But her hands were shaking. So were her legs, in fact. She knew what this was. Low Blood Sugar. The shock of seeing Fred and Jodie cavorting on the field had been too much on an empty stomach. She had to eat something, now.

But Mr Powell had a strict rule about not eating in his office. Jess peered intently at every inch of the ceiling and the walls. There was just no place on earth you could hide a CCTV camera. He'd never know. Jess got out her chocolate milk, and had three delicious gulps – GLUG GLUG GLUG. She felt better already. She put the bottle down on her desk, and got out her pasta salad. It came with a fork and a paper napkin. She opened the plastic container and ate two mouthfuls. It was delicious. Already she felt better.

Then, suddenly, her mobile rang. It was in Mr Powell's desk drawer, but she recognised the horrible raucous ring tone. She must have forgotten to turn it off before handing it over. Even though Mr Powell wasn't there, she felt embarrassed and panicky. With a kind of instinctive lunge, she jumped to her feet.

And as she got up, she jolted her desk, and the open bottle of chocolate milk rocked horribly, perilously – Jess threw out her hand to stop it, but she was still holding the pasta, and instead she knocked the bottle right off the table. It did a kind of somersault and then landed in the middle of Mr Powell's immaculate cream carpet. Glug, glug, glug, went the chocolate milk, flooding out cheerfully in all directions and creating a small lake in which a flotilla of penne pasta floated, thickly coated in tomato sauce.

Jess stared at the carpet in shock and horror. She was tempted to run away and not stop until she came to Scotland, but unfortunately her legs had turned to jelly.

27

THOU SHALT NOT KILL, ALTHOUGH I MIGHT MAKE AN EXCEPTION FOR WASPS

Jess grabbed a handful of tissues and mopped up the worst of the mess, but there was still an enormous brown stain. Mr Powell's cream carpet was ruined. Jess picked up the pieces of pasta. She didn't dare throw them in Mr Powell's waste paper basket, which was immaculate and made of cane. The only place for them was in her bag. But how to protect her books?

Hastily Jess removed one shoe, took off her sock and put all the pasta in there. Then she had an idea. Maybe her socks would be more absorbent than the tissues! She took off the other sock and scrubbed the carpet with it. It had little effect. What she needed was a bucket of carpet shampoo and a sponge.

Jess ran barefoot to the school café. She went

round the back, to where the kitchens were, and asked one of the cooks if she had anything that could work as a carpet cleaner. They looked in the detergent cupboard, but there was nothing actually designed for carpets. The only thing available was a small bowl of washing-up suds and a sponge.

'Thanks very much! You've saved my life!' said Jess, and carried the bowl carefully back to Mr Powell's office. But as she arrived, the most ghastly thing happened. She heard the unmistakable sound of Mr Powell, talking on the phone, inside! He must have come back after all – and been faced with the most horrendous mess in history!

Her heart lurched in terror. She wheeled round and tiptoed away as fast as possible, still carrying the bowl of suds and trying not to spill any. Later Jess would realise that this could form an entertaining event in an alternative Comedy Olympics, but right now she could only form urgent plans to go and live with her father in St Ives.

First, though, she just might hurl the soapsuds over Miss Thorn. If Miss Thorn hadn't been so nasty and inhuman, none of this would have happened.

Jess headed straight for the girls' loos, where she tipped the bowl of soapy water away. A small girl was washing her hands.

'Do me an immense favour and agree to swap lives with me,' said Jess. The little girl looked startled and ran off without answering.

Jess went into the loo at the far end, locked herself in, sat down and dropped her head into her hands. She imagined the sight that must have greeted Mr Powell when he made his unexpected return to his office.

A huge brown stain on his carpet, plus several small red ones (from the pasta). Two socks, one containing penne pasta and one soaked with brown liquid, lying on the floor. Two shoes, probably smelly, just kicked off anywhere. Maybe she could pretend she'd been sick! No, the stain didn't smell right. And that would have been even worse. Or would it? For a minute or two Jess agonised over the respective merits of a lunch that has been hurled over the carpet before being eaten, and one hurled afterwards.

Either way, she was shafted. All her hard work had been ruined. She had tried so hard to be in control. She had followed her schedule religiously. She had attended every lesson on time and done her homework, and the extra work set by Miss Thorn, in beautifully neat handwriting. She had even, in a fit of religious zeal, vacuumed out the inside of her schoolbag.

And now this. Dust and ashes. Or rather chocolate milk and pasta. It was appropriate, somehow, that her downfall had come through food. Satan knows our weaknesses, apparently, and weaves his wicked plans accordingly.

But no. She couldn't really blame Satan. And anyway, she was sure he was far too busy running his worldwide empire to bother with Ashcroft School. Although there was a boy called Jason Cooke in the year above Jess, who was rumoured to be Satan's agent on earth.

From now on, Jess would probably be regarded as spawn of the devil, too. The utter hopelessness of her situation overwhelmed her and she dissolved in tears. She was still crying when she heard the bell go for afternoon lessons. The vague sounds of people coming in and out and going to and fro eventually subsided. She was still crying. She cried and cried and cried.

Eventually she ran out of tears – probably because she hadn't had enough to drink that day – and just kind of slumped against the wall of the loo in a kind of hopeless, helpless stupor. She almost wished Mr Powell and Miss Thorn would come and hunt her down with a pack of bloodthirsty bloodhounds, and tear her to pieces, so it could all be over. Her bare feet were freezing. She took off her jacket and wrapped her feet in it, but then her back started to feel cold.

After a while she started to want to wash her face. The tears had dried, leaving an unpleasant salty stretchy feeling. Thank goodness she hadn't been wearing any mascara, because of being On Report. She let herself out of the cubicle and went over to the washbasins. There was a mirror by the hand drier. Jess could not believe how awful she looked. Her eyes had turned into raw meat.

She was washing her face when the bell rang for the end of lessons. People came into the loo, cheerful and noisy because it was Friday. Jess ignored them. Then she heard a familiar voice.

'Jess!' It was Jodie. 'Where are your shoes? Are you OK?'

'Not really,' said Jess, leaning on the washbasin.

'Have you been sick?' asked Jodie. 'What colour was it?'

How could Fred spend the lunch hour kissing the hand of a girl who cared about the colour of vomit?

'No, it's not that,' said Jess. 'Get Flora over here, will you? Right now.'

'But we've got a runthrough of *Twelfth Night*.'

'Just for five minutes. I've got to see her.'

Jodie ran off, and Jess went back down to the cubicles – a more secluded corner. She didn't want to be visible in case Miss Thorn walked past and looked in. One of the lessons Jess had missed this afternoon was English. If Jason Cooke was indeed Satan's representative at school, he was certainly doing just fine and would probably be awarded a star.

'Jess?' she heard Flora's voice call from out by the door.

'In here!' called Jess. Luckily the loos were almost empty now – everybody had left. Flora appeared, looking anxious. At the sight of Jess she bit her lip, looked shocked and held out her arms like a mother.

'Jess! Babe! What's the matter?'

Jess collapsed in Flora's fragrant embrace and wept all over again – quite copiously, all over Flora's shoulder and into her hair.

'Oh God! Oh God! I'm sorry! I'm in the worst trouble ever!'

'Tell me!'

Jess embarked on the whole story.

'Last night – last night my mum told me she's having an affair.'

'What! With a married man?'

'I don't think he's married. It's her pupil – Mr Nishizawa. He's almost young enough to be her son!

If she was our age, he'd only be two! Imagine it!'

They both imagined the horror of having a boyfriend whose only small talk was *Wanna bikkit!* and *Teddy says boo!*

Jess resumed her tragic tale: the missed breakfast, the low blood sugar, the glimpse of Fred kissing Jodie's hand, the panic attack, and the race to Mr Powell's office. The desperate, on-the-point-of-fainting hunger, the horrid phone ringing in the drawer (that would have been Satan, obviously), and then the ghastly, ghastly moment when the chocolate milk had taken to the air. The spill, the clearing-up panic, the race to the kitchen, and then the most agonising moment of all, the sound of Mr Powell's voice in his office, and the realisation that he had come back.

'And since then,' said Jess, 'I've been crying for England in the end loo, all afternoon. So I've missed three more lessons.'

Naturally this saga took a long time to explain. Jess provided additional reasons why her emotional state was so terribly fragile right now. There was the awful way Mackenzie was trying to hijack her comedy show.

'Mackenzie is a total control freak,' agreed Flora with a shudder. 'He was like that when we were going out.'

241

And then there was the painful misunderstanding with Fred. Jess confessed she had literally NO IDEA whether he still liked her or not, but she had run out of hope. She had run out of everything: courage, self-belief. And she had run out of tears. Again.

'First thing you must do,' said Flora, 'is go to Mr Powell. Now. Or it'll be torturing you all weekend.'

'Come with me!' pleaded Jess. A look of furtive terror flashed briefly over Flora's face.

'I can't, Jess! I'm supposed to be at a runthrough right now! I'm twenty minutes – no ...' she glanced at her watch, and gasped, 'no – half an hour late! Oh God! I've gotta go, babe – but listen – go to Mr Powell now, and just apologise for England.'

'I'd rather die,' said Jess. 'Anyway, he's probably gone.'

'Take my advice,' said Flora, 'and go to his office.'

'I'll wait for you, till you've finished your run-through,' said Jess.

'No, Jess – it'll take hours. Just go and see Mr Powell and fess up. It's the only way. Crawl and grovel and offer to do all sorts of remedial thingies. That's what I do with my dad. And do it with captivating feminine charm. That always works on Dad. I stroke his hair. It never fails.'

'I can't stroke Mr Powell's hair, for God's sake!' A

horrible hallucination flashed through Jess's mind.

'No, but – you know, he'll be waiting for you, probably!' Flora looked at her watch again and went pale. 'I have to go. Sorry, babe. But I'm majorly late.'

Flora went. Jess washed her face again. She had never looked less attractive. It would take her two hours' intensive work with cosmetics to come anywhere near to radiating captivating feminine charm. All the same, she did understand Flora's advice. She had reached some kind of crunch point. All the lies in the world wouldn't get her off this hook. She simply had to go to see Mr Powell – now.

28

WEAR NOT THE STILETTO HEEL LEST YE RUIN THY NEIGHBOUR'S PARQUET

Jess walked to Mr Powell's office, her legs shaking and her feet frozen on the cold stones of the corridor. She knocked softly on the door, praying ardently for him to be out.

'Come in!'

She opened the door and crept in. The first thing she saw was the carpet. It was immaculately clean. For a moment she thought it had all been a bad dream. Then she glanced over to the desk where she had sat, and there was her school bag. There was a plastic bag lying on the desk containing her murdered socks. At last she raised her eyes to Mr Powell. She must look like one of those dogs which has led a life of abuse and stares sullenly up with doleful eyes, expecting punishment.

'I'm sorry,' she croaked. 'I'm so, so sorry.'

Mr Powell regarded her soberly from his desk. His fingers were steepled, the fingertips touching his lips, as if in prayer.

Her face twitched madly, longing to cry again. So much for captivating feminine charm.

'I've been crying all afternoon in the girls' loos,' she went on, her voice quavering madly like an old lady in a cartoon. 'I missed my lessons, I'm sorry. I'll never do this kind of thing ever again. Living like this is no good. It's insane.'

The ghost of a smile flickered across Mr Powell's lips. A *smile*. He unsteepled his fingers and brushed an imaginary speck of dust off his desk.

'You're a very lucky girl,' he said. 'My wife gave birth at lunchtime to a boy, so I'm in a very good mood. So good that nothing can spoil it. Not even a foul and disgusting mess like the one you left.'

'I was coming back with a bucket of soapy water,' said Jess. 'Then I heard your voice and I couldn't face you. I ran away. I was scared to death.'

'I was at the hospital at lunchtime,' said Mr Powell. 'So what you heard must have been the outgoing message on my answering machine.'

Jess's heart sank. If she hadn't been in such a rush earlier she would have realised it wasn't really Mr

Powell, and gone in and cleaned up.

'So I'm frightening, am I?' said Mr Powell. What an odd conversation this was.

'Very, very frightening indeed,' Jess assured him.

'How very reassuring,' said Mr Powell.

'Even more frightening than God,' Jess went on. 'His beard makes him look kind of cuddly.'

'I won't grow a beard, then,' said Mr Powell.

'What are you going to call the baby?' asked Jess.

'Dan,' said Mr Powell.

'A lovely name!' said Jess. 'Manly. What does he weigh?' Grown-ups always ask that question. What else is there to say about a baby?

'Eight and a half pounds!' said Mr Powell, with evident pride.

'My God!' said Jess. 'A whopper! Congratulations.'

'Thank you,' said Mr Powell.

There was a moment's silence. Jess did not want to push her luck, so she waited for him to make the next move, with just the hint of a captivatingly feminine but deeply remorseful smile on her horrid blotchy face.

'You've caught me at quite a mellow moment,' said Mr Powell. 'You're a lucky girl. I shall be on paternity leave starting on Monday. I've just nipped back now to clear my desk.' He stared at Jess in a thoughtful way. 'I think I'll have to put you On Report for another week,' he said. 'Or possibly a fortnight. But you'll have to report to Mrs Tomkins's office.'

'Of course,' said Jess. She would gladly be On Report for the rest of her life. And though Mr Powell's shouting could remove roof tiles, Mrs Tomkins, though theoretically his superior, was a bit of a pussycat really.

'You can go now,' he said. 'I put your socks in that plastic bag.'

'Thank you,' said Jess. She picked up her bag and slipped into her shoes. Then she paused for a moment and stared at the carpet in fascination. It was completely clean – though you could tell it had been treated.

'Yes,' said Mr Powell. 'You're lucky, as I said. I'm probably the only Head of Year in the country with a bottle of carpet shampoo in my drawer. It's called Carpet Devil.'

Satan would approve.

'I'm a little bit obsessive that way. In fact ...' he pulled out his drawer and placed the carpet shampoo on his desk, '... I suppose I'd better take it home with me. We'll be needing it a lot more often now.'

Then another thought occurred to him. He pulled out another drawer and handed Jess her phone.

'It's been ringing, so I switched it off,' he said.

Jess accepted it gratefully, and put it away in her bag straight away, without looking to see whose calls she had missed.

'It was the phone that caused the accident,' she said. 'It rang in the drawer and I –'

'Don't bore me with the sordid details,' said Mr Powell, picking up his own phone. 'Off you go now. Report to Mrs Tomkins first thing on Monday.'

Jess almost skipped out of his office. Mr Powell was such a darling! Under the hideous yelling monsterhood he was such a sweetie-pie! And however cross he was with her in future, it would be OK, because he had secretly been nice to her, and you could never forget a thing like that. She knew about his cute baby called Dan! Why, they were almost bosom chums.

Jess checked the phone, hoping it would be a text from Fred saying something like: **WHY AREN'T YOU IN ENGLISH? THE WORLD HAS TURNED TO DUST AND ASHES WITHOUT YOU. FLY BACK TO MY ARMS OR I'LL PUNCH YOU IN THE MOUTH.** But there was nothing from Fred. Only a couple of ads from the mobile phone company.

But the wonderful redemption of the scene with Mr Powell was encouraging. She was sure that if such a horrid situation could come right, she and Fred would surely be reconciled again somehow. She felt, for the first time, full of hope.

She didn't even mind that Mum and Nori had gone to the Peak District. She hoped they would have lots of lovely bracing walks, and return to their hotel too tired to do anything more than fall instantly asleep. Jess walked home feeling more positive than she had felt for a long time, and looking forward to her weekend with Granny.

It started well. Granny was in a good mood and made a simple but festive dish called cinnamon toast. They had just settled down to watch *Murder, She Wrote*, when the doorbell rang.

'I'll get it!' cried Jess, leaping up. Who knew, it might even be Fred? And if it was Mackenzie and Ben, she'd tell them she had a headache. She opened the door. It was Flora. In floods of tears.

'Guess what!' she sobbed. 'I've been thrown out of the play! Miss Thorn said I'd kept everybody waiting for half an hour, and I was totally unreliable, and she just went horrible and icy and cold, and told me to leave!'

29

IF SEVEN WISE VIRGINS COME TO THY DOOR, PRETEND THOU ART OUT AND HIDE TILL THEY TIRE OF KNOCKING

A tidal wave of guilt washed over Jess. She'd been so desperate about her own troubles she had hardly been aware that Flora was supposed to be at a run-through. Flora had been there for her, with comfort and advice. And this was her reward. Thrown out of the play for being a good mate.

'Come in!' she said, pulling Flora indoors. 'It's only Flora!' she called to Granny, who was deep into TV murder. 'Come upstairs!' said Jess, and they went up to her room, where Flora continued her crying fit, lying on the bed and hanging on to Rasputin. Teddy bears are great for tinies, but they really come into their own when you reach your teens.

'I haven't told my dad!' she sobbed. 'I can't face it! He'll give me such a hard time! My mum was so disappointed, she had tears in her eyes!'

'Did you ...' Jess ventured. 'Did you tell her it was because of me?' She was afraid Flora's mum would hate her for ruining her daughter's career.

'Yes, well, I had to explain why I'd been so late,' said Flora. 'But Mum's cool about that, she was sorry you'd been so upset. She just thinks Miss Thorn is a cold-hearted bitch. She thinks she should just have told me off or put me on a warning or something.'

'God, I'm sorry!' said Jess. 'I'm so, so, sorry. What can I do to make it all right again?'

Flora was coming to the end of her cry now. She sat up and sniffed and tried to breathe normally.

'Pass me a tissue, please, babe,' she said. Jess obliged. Flora blew her nose. 'I don't blame you at all,' Flora went on. 'I knew I would be a bit late, but I never dreamt she'd throw me out.'

'Thorn is a cow,' said Jess with venom. 'She's totally overreacted.'

'The thing is,' said Flora, 'she's shouted at me a couple of times in rehearsal, for whispering to Jack, and I forgot my script once, and she went ballistic. And I kept forgetting things – you know, moves and stuff. I got the feeling she was almost looking for an excuse to dump me.'

'It's because you're my friend, as well,' said Jess. 'She hates me like poison. But never mind. We'll have our revenge,' she said. Flora looked apprehensive.

'What are you planning?' she asked. 'I mean – she's such a dragon, it might be best just to keep out of her way.'

'I've got to get back at her,' said Jess. 'Somehow. And I will.'

Flora winced and rubbed her tummy.

'Ow!' she said. 'Cramps. Oh no. And they're going to get worse. I'd better ring my sister and ask her to come and fetch me.'

Flora rang her sister, and Jess made her a hot water bottle. While they waited for Freya, Flora lay on Jess's bed and groaned from time to time.

'How was Irritable Powell? You did go and see him, didn't you?' asked Flora, between cramps.

'Yeah, I did …' Jess hesitated. 'Thank God you told me to, because he was almost OK about it. He said I'd have to go back on report for a bit longer, but he was amazingly mellow, really. His wife had just had a baby. Today.'

'I'm never going to have a baby,' said Flora. 'Not if this is what it feels like. My mum says labour pains are quite like period pains only worse.' She winced again. Jess stroked her hair. She hardly ever had pains of any sort. She felt lucky. Though fear of insanity was a major concern, of course.

Soon Flora's sister came and took her away, and she was as friendly to Jess as ever, thank goodness. But Jess still felt terrible. Being in that play had meant so much to Flora. How could Miss Thorn be such a vindictive cow?

On Monday morning Jess would get to school early, go and see Miss Thorn and beg her to change her mind. She would say it was all her fault that Flora had been late. Maybe she could get her to reconsider. But Flora had already told Miss Thorn all this, and it hadn't worked. Jess knew how unwelcome her presence was to Miss Thorn. She suspected she would only make matters worse.

She went downstairs and made herself a cup of hot chocolate. Granny waddled into the kitchen.

'I've had an orgy of serial murder this evening,' she sighed happily. 'It's been wonderful, dear. And now all I need is a milky drink. I should have an early night, but there's an old *Prime Suspect* on at 9.30, so I might just stay up for that. I love *Prime Suspect*. The police are even more repulsive than the criminals.'

She put some milk in a saucepan and got out her

253

favourite post-murder night-time drink. Jess stared at the kitchen table, her head in her hands. She remembered how happy and relaxed she had felt earlier in the evening. Since Flora had come round, she now felt more deeply depressed than ever before. Guilt really was the pits.

'Are you all right, dear?' asked Granny. 'You look a bit down.'

Jess opened her mouth to reassure Granny: the doorbell rang. Granny looked startled.

'Whoever can that be at this time of night?' she said. It was only about eight o'clock, but at this end of the summer the evenings soon became gloomy.

'Well, if it's a serial killer, I'll refer him to you, Granny,' said Jess, getting up and walking to the door. She had an awful looming kind of dread that it was Miss Thorn, coming round to make a scene. Or Mackenzie, intent on showing her how he could present the comedy show in the character of Bugs Bunny. She opened the door, therefore, with an aggressive sneer ready and waiting.

But it was Fred. Jess was absolutely stunned. The one time she had not been expecting or hoping for a visit. She had given up hope, in fact.

'Who is it, dear?' called Granny from the kitchen.

'It's only Fred!' said Jess.

'Oh, good,' said Granny, toddling down the hall carrying her milky drink. 'We haven't seen Fred for ages. Come in, dear!'

Thank goodness Granny was able to perform the necessary hospitable acts, because Jess's heart was hammering so hard she couldn't say a word to him. Fred was also silent, but he stepped inside and Jess closed the door behind him.

'How are you, Fred, my dear?' beamed Granny.

'Fine, thank you, Mrs Collins,' said Fred.

'Good boy! You're so tall! How tall are you now?'

'Five eleven and three quarters,' said Fred. 'Mustn't boast.'

'Goodness me! You'll end up well over six foot, I'm sure. I do like a man to be tall. That's something I don't quite like about Mr Thingumajig.' She turned to Jess. 'I don't mind him being Japanese, and he's got lovely manners, but he's only about five foot seven.'

'Yes, it is a goddam cheek,' agreed Jess. 'Tell you what, let's shoot him as soon as they get back.'

Granny chuckled. 'I've decided to retire to my sty,' she said. 'I'm going to get into bed and if I'm still awake at nine thirty, I'll watch *Prime Suspect* on my little telly in there.'

'Jolly good, Granny, go for it, wallow in homicide.'

Granny gave a funny little wave to Fred.

'Give Fred a cup of coffee, dear, and a slice of my lemon drizzle cake.'

Then Granny went into her room and shut the door. Though usually Jess longed to be alone with Fred, this time she felt nervous. She almost wished Granny had stayed up to prattle on. She couldn't think of a single thing to say.

'Apparently I've got to offer you food and drink,' she said. 'Would you like to go into the kitchen?' And she made a flamboyant *after you* sort of gesture.

Why didn't he just sweep her into his arms, the fool? On the other hand, why had he put her through all this, the swine? Waves of passion surged through Jess: absolute adoration followed immediately by downright rage. It was going to be a stormy night.

30

THE CAMEL SEES NOT ITS OWN HUMP NOR DOES IT SAY 'DOES MY HUMP LOOK BIG IN THIS?'

Fred pushed open the kitchen door gingerly, as if he was afraid someone was in there.

'My mum's gone to the Peak District with her Japanese toyboy,' said Jess.

'It's not your mum I'm worried about,' said Fred. 'Last time I was here Ben Jones was in charge, offering me stuff and acting as if he owned the place.'

He went into the kitchen with a disgusted look, as if some kind of faint whiff of Ben Jones was still hanging about in the air.

'Oh, you're not jealous of *him*!' said Jess, in exasperation.

'Why not?' said Fred. 'Offering me a Coke, the bastard. And my mum said you and he were holding hands in the Dolphin Café, on the first day of term.'

'We weren't holding hands! We were arm-wrestling! And if you hadn't been absent I'd have been able to arm-wrestle with you – although, let's face it, with a nerd like you there'd have been no contest.'

There was a moment of silence. Jess summoned every tiny scrap of courage. She had to keep the show on the road.

'Why have you waited till now to come?' she demanded angrily. 'Why didn't you come before?'

'When we met at the Health Centre,' said Fred, 'I thought you'd borrowed my hoodie to give me an excuse to come round and get it back, so we could talk. So I come round – conquering my overpowering urge to run away and hide under a large stone – and what do I find? Jones in full possession of your kitchen, lounging about with his blonde hair gleaming seductively in the romantic halogen downlighters. And then to crown it all, it appears that it was his football shorts you were waltzing about in at school.'

'Oh, don't be such a retard!' snapped Jess. 'Ben lent me his shorts because I'd sat down on a mud slick on the school field. He came round to get them back. Earlier we'd done some mild arm-wrestling. So what? If you hadn't been hiding and running off and avoiding me, I would have been too busy giving you a hard time to spend a single moment with him.'

'One cannot compete with Ben Jones,' shrugged Fred. 'One fears him as the wildebeest fears the lion.'

'Lion, my arse!' said Jess. 'He's more like a three-toed sloth. And anyway, while we're on the subject, you're the one who's been misbehaving. You've been flirting fit to bust, and kissing people, the lot.'

'Kissing?' Fred looked puzzled. 'The lot? I certainly haven't kissed anybody at all, let alone, God forbid – indulged in *the lot*.'

'I saw you, you moron!' cried Jess. 'Kissing Jodie on the school field. Today!'

Fred's face cleared. 'We were just rehearsing,' he said. 'She's the Countess Olivia, I'm her steward. We've got scenes together. And we're so scared of Thorn, we practise together. I've also got a scene with David Green and we practise that too.'

At this point the kettle boiled, and Jess made two cups of coffee. She secretly preferred hot chocolate, but she felt she might need a little extra demonic energy this evening. Fred was still standing up, looking as if he might leave at any moment. Jess got Grandma's cake out of a plastic box and cut him a huge slice.

'Sit down,' she said. She pushed the plate across the table towards him. The smell of the lemon was very alluring. Fred sat down, stirred his coffee, and looked at the cake with a kind of distant admiration.

'Can't quite manage the cake yet,' he said. 'Too terrified to eat.'

'Terrified?' said Jess. 'Of what?'

'Well, of you, of course. As you know, cowardice is the bedrock of my character. It's taken me hours to summon up the courage to come here. I even had to have a Vitamin C tablet.'

'So why did you come?' asked Jess. 'Why today?'

'When Flora was explaining to Thorn why she'd been late, she said you'd been, er … *upset* was the word she used. Shortly before Thorn gave her what I believe is known as "the bum's rush" and ejected her from the play.'

'So you were worried that I'd been upset?'

'I thought you must have been quite spectacularly upset for Flora to be so late, I mean, for a runthrough and everything.'

Jess was deeply touched.

'I didn't know you cared,' she said, archly, to hide her delight.

'Oh, I don't, of course, as you know,' said Fred. 'I came more in the spirit of ghoulish tourism, the way that people drive slowly past road accidents.'

'Well, I hope you're satisfied,' said Jess, cruelly aware that she had not bothered to apply mascara or lippy since arriving home, assuming that it would only be her and Granny having a girls' night in. 'My face is, of course, hideously blotched with weeping. In fact, I have never looked so vile.'

'Oh, I don't know…' Fred looked at her across the table, and his eyes began to sparkle. 'I can remember days when you looked even worse.'

Immense relief flooded through Jess's heart. Things were beginning to get back to normal. But she still had to try and understand how they'd got into such a mess in the first place.

'Just explain one thing to me,' she said. 'Why did you say such a horrid thing to me, back there in the park? That you wanted to pretend we were deadly enemies? Some joke!'

Fred looked tortured.

'Don't let's even go there,' he said, cringing and kind of ducking at the memory of it. 'I was just really nervous, in a pathetic nerdy way, I admit, about going back to school. I hate being looked at, as you know.'

'*You* hate being looked at?' said Jess. 'You're the biggest show-off in the class.'

'Well, I mean, I knew the guys would kind of –

give me a hard time.'

'My heart bleeds for you,' said Jess scathingly. 'I, on the other hand, was so thrilled to be going out with you that I couldn't wait to tell my mates and collect the envious congratulations.' She really was quite disappointed in Fred.

'Yeah, well …' said Fred. 'I was just embarrassed, you know. I didn't want … I wouldn't have wanted to be like Flora and Mackenzie when they were going out together, sort of snogging and pawing each other all day.'

'But we would never have behaved like that anyway!' said Jess. 'We're cool, remember? Withdrawn, enigmatic, mysterious.'

'Oh yeah,' said Fred. 'So we are. I'm sorry. Anyway, once you'd gone off in a huff –'

'It was not a huff!' cried Jess. 'My heart was broken, you moron!'

'Once you'd gone off with heartbreak, etc,' said Fred, 'I became suddenly terrified. I was sure you'd never speak to me again. You know I was away on the first day of school?'

'Yes – why was that? I was so desperate to see you I almost died.'

'Well, I was so desperate *not* to see you because of feeling so guilty,' said Fred. 'I couldn't face you, I hadn't slept, my life was in ruins, etc, so I went off and sat in the park all day. Under our tree. In torment. But why didn't you come to school the next morning? Was it because you couldn't face me?'

'Of course I could face you, you cretin!' said Jess. 'Don't judge everybody by your own cowardly standards. I had to have the morning off because I hadn't done my homework, that's all. So I feigned vomiting. It was an Oscar-winning performance, though I say so myself.'

'Oh,' said Fred. 'Well, good.' He stared back down at the cake. 'I think I could manage a piece of this cake now.'

'It's a damn fine cake,' said Jess, getting stuck into her own, smaller piece.

They ate their cake in silence, but it was a good silence.

'By the way,' said Jess, 'why did you go to the Health Centre that time? What was wrong with you? Something serious, I hope?'

'Athlete's foot,' said Fred. 'Ironical, really, for someone who avoids exercise at all costs.'

'Fungus the Bogeyman, eh?' said Jess with a smile. 'Extremely attractive little detail, that.'

'After we've finished our cake,' said Fred, 'I'd like to come round the other side of the table and give you a hug. But of course I realise I haven't earned it yet.'

Jess was surprised. She would have been quite happy to have a hug from Fred in any circumstances.

'The thing is,' said Fred, 'I know my cowardice is deeply unattractive. Even if it's not loathsome to you, it certainly disgusts me. So in order to earn your renewed affection – if indeed you are considering renewing it – I have an offer.'

'An offer?' Jess felt uneasy. She hoped he wasn't going to ask her to marry him. Though she had often fantasised about a life by the sea with Fred and twins called Freda and Freddo, plus a range of cute dogs of all sizes, it would be kind of tacky if he proposed to her now. She might just *really* go off him.

'Set me any impossible task,' said Fred. 'Name it, I'll do it. I kind of have to prove to myself that my spine does exist and is made of bone, not butter. So set me an impossible task, and I will earn your good will. Like a knight of old type thing. Don't send me off on a crusade, though – it's terribly politically incorrect these days, and besides, I can't stand spicy food.'

Jess was amazed by this offer, and thought for a minute. She was glad Fred found his own cowardice repulsive, because she had to admit she didn't much like it herself. It's horrible when you love somebody but there's something about them which puts you off. She had been quite perturbed by Fred's account of his fears. And as it happened, there was one thing which she felt very strongly about right now.

'OK,' she said. 'Leave *Twelfth Night*.'

'What?' Fred went pale.

'Tell Miss Thorn you don't want to be in the play,' said Jess.

'Not be in the play?' Fred was deeply shocked. You could tell by his shortage of words.

'You've got to admit that for Thorn to throw Flora out is deeply unfair,' said Jess.

'Yeah. It stinks,' agreed Fred.

'All Flora did was look after me when I was in a terrible state today. I've never cried so much in a single day before. I felt quite thirsty afterwards. And one of the reasons I was so upset was because of you.'

'Yes,' said Fred, still deathly pale. 'OK.'

'And Flora was so thrilled to be in *Twelfth Night*, and now she's been dropped she's absolutely desperate. She was here earlier, weeping bucketloads. She hasn't even dared to tell her dad yet. So, to show your bravery, and your loyalty to me and my friend, I want you to drop out of *Twelfth Night*. Because the woman organising it is a bitch and she has behaved unjustly

265

to my friend. OK?'

Fred took a deep breath, swallowed a couple of times and stared at his hands, which were shaking. Then he looked up at Jess and raised his eyebrow in a quirky manner.

'There isn't … something slightly less terrifying I could do, is there?'

31

MARRY NOT AN AGEING ROCK STAR: THOU WOULDST BE THOUGHT A BRAINLESS GOLD-DIGGER

On Monday, Jess and Fred resumed their habit of walking to school together. At Flora's house they paused.

'I'll just find out if she's coming to school today,' said Jess. 'She had period pains yesterday.'

At the dreaded words *period pains* Fred went pale and backed off down the pavement.

'I'd hate to interrupt your girly gossip about gonads and stuff,' he said. 'I think I'll make an excuse and leave. See you at lunchtime.'

'Yeah,' said Jess. 'Although I don't intend to speak to you until you've done the decent thing and broken Thorny's heart in two by your shock resignation.' Fred kind of shuddered and pulled an agonised face.

'You can do it,' said Jess. 'You're my hero.'

'Couldn't I be your terrified pet mouse instead?' said Fred.

'No,' said Jess. 'The time has come for you to prove your manhood.'

'Uhhh – guess what, I think I left it at home,' said Fred. Then he pulled up his hood and walked off. He looked scared – *really* scared.

Jess went in to collect Flora and impart the fantastic news that Fred was back in her life. Flora was pleased, and gave Jess a hug, but she was preoccupied with her own problems and looking more beautiful than ever in a kind of picturesquely disgraced way. Last night she had plucked up her courage and told her dad she'd been thrown out of the play.

'Dad surprised me,' she confided, as they turned into the main road. 'He just said that was OK, because I'd have more time for maths homework.'

Flora's dad could be a bit of a philistine sometimes. He regarded the arts as something people got involved with if they didn't have anything important to do.

When they got to school, Jess reported to Mrs Tomkins's office. Mrs Tomkins was busy on the phone so she just waved Jess to a desk in the corner of her room. Her office had lots of pictures of the Tomkins family windsurfing, and there were flowers on the desk. It was also a lot cosier and untidier than Mr Powell's office.

'Right, Jess,' said Mrs Tomkins briskly, when she finished her call, 'I gather you're On Report for a week, so get on with it. I hope by the time we get to Friday you'll be a reformed character.'

Mrs Tomkins tried to look stern, but succeeded only in looking not quite as jolly as usual. She found it hard to be cross with Jess, because her mother was a librarian. Jess assured her that she was deeply penitent, and resumed her scholarly endeavours. From now on, she would be so saintly the Pope might need to be informed.

After school Flora was waiting in the Dolphin, and Mackenzie and Ben were with her, eager to talk about the comedy show. But there was, as yet, no sign of Fred. He hadn't managed to see Miss Thorn at lunchtime, because she was busy rehearsing (luckily, not one of his scenes), so he'd had to have his showdown with her after school. Right now, he was probably telling her he was withdrawing from the play. If he chickened out, Jess was determined to have another massive row with him, this time lasting months.

'So how was your day, babe?' she asked Flora. Jess still felt desperately guilty that her crisis last Friday had caused Flora so much heartache.

'Actually, it's been fantastic,' said Flora. 'I've never spent a day being bad before. In disgrace. It's quite glamorous.'

'But you're not bad!' said Jess. 'You're being punished because you're *good*, remember?'

'Oh, but it's almost as good as being bad,' said Flora. 'People were coming up to me all day and were like, *I hear you've been chucked out of the play*. I had this kind of feeling, you know, kind of criminal chic. I may even defy my dad and have my nose pierced.'

'Well, you're on a downhill path,' said Jess. 'With luck you could avoid your dreadful destiny at Oxford University and head for a women's prison instead.'

'Anyway,' said Mackenzie, really annoyingly, as if everything everyone had said so far was irrelevant and time-wasting and he was really in charge, 'now you're not in the play you can be in our comedy show.'

Jess nearly hit him.

'I've had a great idea,' Mackenzie went on. 'I could present the show as Jerry Springer.'

'I'll just get myself a massive snack,' said Jess,

getting up and going to the counter. She was so tempted to bite Mackenzie she would just have to sink her teeth into a sandwich instead. How was she going to deal with Mackenzie and make him realise he was *not* in charge of the show? And what if Fred didn't show up? What if he had bottled out?

However, two minutes later, Jess had just taken an enormous mouthful of a BLT roll when Fred walked in. He looked a little pale, but his eyes glittered strangely. He threw himself down into a chair and looked directly at Jess.

'Well,' he said, 'I'm not in *Twelfth Night* either, as of now.'

'You *what*?' said Flora, astonished.

'I gave in my notice,' said Fred, 'to show solidarity, and so forth, and express my disgust at the way you were treated on Friday. Acting on instructions from my captain here.' He nodded at Jess. His captain! This was by far the best moment of the term.

'I'm proud of you, Parsons,' said Jess in a US Marine Commander's voice. 'You'll get the red star for courage, the white star for an excellent haircut under fire … heck, you'll get every star in the goddam firmament.'

'Sir!' said Fred, saluting.

'You did this for me?' gasped Flora, tactfully turning

271

to Jess, to avoid any suggestion that it was Fred's idea, and that Flora was so touched she might fall in love with Fred (*again* – there was a little bit of history there).

'Yes,' said Jess. 'Well, the way Thorny treated you, she deserves everything she gets. But hey, Fred – what did you say to Thorn? Did she blow you away?'

'The details of our interview must remain private,' said Fred, with a nervous grimace. 'Anyway, she's got Luke Harding now. He was my understudy, and now his moment has come. His nose was certainly created with comedy in mind.'

'He'll be rubbish compared to you,' said Flora.

'And whatshername with the red hair will be rubbish compared to you, dear lady,' said Fred.

'Anyway,' said Mackenzie, 'the great thing is that now you can be in our comedy show too.'

'It's kind of – Fred's show anyway, Mac, you prat,' said Ben Jones quickly – by his standards. 'He's like, written all the material so far and he and Jess were planning to do it – uh, ages ago.'

Jess gave Ben a smile. He was such a darling! Then her attention was distracted by somebody coming into the café. It was Jack Stevens, the amazingly handsome guy who was playing Orsino in *Twelfth*

Night. He walked straight up to their table and looked right at Flora.

'I'm really gutted you're not in the play any more,' he said. Flora went bright red. 'That woman is a nightmare,' he went on. 'You were brilliant. It's rubbish without you.'

Flora smiled, but her heart was beating so fast you could see the pulse in her neck. She opened her mouth, but no words came out: her lips trembled.

'Yeah!' said Jess, leaping to her rescue. 'You're so right. Thorny is a monster. Wanna Coke?' She leant back and dragged an extra chair over from the next table, and placed it between her and Flora. Jack Stevens joined them so eagerly Jess just knew he fancied Flora. Who wouldn't?

'I'll get some more drinks,' said Fred, and went off to the counter. Jess joined him.

'I see the demon lover has come up trumps,' said Fred, buying a few more bottles. 'Almost illegally good-looking, isn't he, the great big show-off?'

'Shut up, Fred,' giggled Jess. 'This is the best thing that's happened to Flora for ages. She hasn't had a boyfriend since Mackenzie, and even then, the person she really had a crush on was you.'

'Don't remind me,' said Fred, paying at the till. 'That was a narrow escape. Phew! Worse than *Jaws*.'

They went back to the table, where Mackenzie was arguing with Ben, and Jack was staring intently into Flora's eyes as if longing to sweep her into his manly arms. Flora had evidently thought of something to say to him, and she had never looked prettier. Fred passed round the drinks and sat down.

'Right,' said Mackenzie. 'This is a kind of meeting about our comedy show, so let's get on. I've had some fantastic ideas. I'm going to present it as Jerry Springer.'

Fred looked swiftly at Jess, and knew instantly what she was thinking.

'No, I think Jess should present it, actually, old boy,' said Fred. 'Argue with me at your peril. Jess is going to present it – as Miss Thorn.'

'Miss Thorn!' gasped Jess. 'Fantastic idea!'

'But …' Flora hesitated. 'Won't she, like, get really cross, and won't it be, well, a bit risky?'

'She deserves it!' said Jess. 'It's a brilliant idea, Fred. *Sit still – yes, I mean YOU! And there is to be no tiresome laughing.*' Everybody cracked up.

'That's amazing! It sounds just like her!' said Flora. 'And we could make you look quite like her, actually. All we need is a power suit and make your hair into a kind of sleek bob, and the eyebrows, well – you're queen of the eyebrow pencil anyway.'

'You've really got her voice,' said Jack in amazement. 'How do you do it?'

'Miss Thorn could go on the *Jerry Springer Show*,' said Mackenzie. 'She could, like, lose it and start fighting with her ex.'

'Shut up about Jerry Springer,' said Fred, 'or I may have to slightly murder you. If you want to appear as a star of stage and screen, may I suggest – Frodo Baggins?'

'And you can shut up about Frodo Baggins,' said Mackenzie. 'I'm not that small. I'm five foot eight for God's sake.'

Nobody said anything for a moment, and they all avoided eye contact. Mackenzie was *so not* five eight.

'Look, we're not saying you're a Hobbit,' said Jess patiently. 'Just get back in your matchbox and stop trying to control everything. Fred's the producer/director now, OK? What he says, goes.'

'OK,' said Fred. 'Let's make a list of ideas, yeah? I'll put Jerry Springer down, just to keep Mackenzie happy. But we can always rule it out later.'

He looked round with a charming smile, and got a pen and a notebook out of his bag. Jess felt a great surge of joy. Jack Stevens had arrived to cheer Flora up. And the comedy show was going to be terrific. She was going to take the piss out of Miss Thorn, quite mercilessly. She'd have the whole school laughing at her. And it would feel fabulous. The revenge she'd been longing for was right here in her hands, and who cared about the consequences?

32

A FOOL AND HIS MONEY ARE SOON PARTED, BUT REMEMBER THY FATHER HATH NONE IN THE FIRST PLACE

After another week with Mrs Tomkins, Jess rejoined normal lessons. She was intrigued by the way Miss Thorn just ignored her completely. In fact, Jess, Flora and Fred might just as well have been totally invisible. She marked their work, and gave them grades, but never asked them questions in class – never even looked at them. To Jess, this was a sign that Miss Thorn was majorly upset. It was a triumph.

Jess watched Miss Thorn closely. She noticed every little habit. Miss Thorn had a way of rubbing her thumb against her index finger. She also had a way of glaring at somebody which included a flash of the whites of the eyes. She sometimes pursed her lips like someone who has just sucked a lemon.

And Jess listened avidly to her voice. There was a kind of tinny edge to it, as if she was deliberately making it into a thin whine. Jess practised all this at home in front of the bathroom mirror. She was writing the script for Miss Thorn's introduction of the comedy show, and her appearance between sketches which linked things together and gave the others time for quick costume changes when necessary.

Miss Thorn had a number of catchphrases which Jess thought might be useful. She made a list. *Be quiet!* (That one came out like the bark of a yappy little dog.) *You've not come here to enjoy yourselves. As you can see, nobody's amused. If I hear the slightest whisper you'll all be here after school. Ah, another doomed attempt at humour.* It seemed as if Miss Thorn had a hang-up about laughter. The script practically wrote itself.

Jess had a bit of a problem inventing a name for her, though. At first she turned over dozens of harsh, vicious names. Jacqueline Scratch. Martha Murgatroyd. Harriet Steel.

But then she happened to be ransacking the kitchen drawer – looking for a plastic bag to wrap her ingredients for the home economics lesson – and she caught sight of a pile of old leaflets and guarantees for various kitchen appliances. And one was called the Sunbeam.

A perfect name for Miss Thorn! Of course, irony was much better than giving a vicious person a vicious name. Miss Sunbeam. Fantastic. Jess tried to think of a soft, gentle first name for her. Ah! Susie.

'I'm calling her Susie Sunbeam,' she said to the gang when they met at Fred's that night. They all thought it was perfect.

'And, hey, it's got – uh, illiteracy,' said Ben Jones.

'Alliteration, Ben, you primitive life form,' said Jess. She abused him to his face now in front of Fred – and she got the feeling Ben liked it. 'Illiteracy is something else.'

The weeks passed, and the show took shape. There was a sketch called The Pointless Olympics. Events included Picking the Nose Whilst Standing on One Leg, Trying Not to Cry Whilst Thinking of Puppies Being Ill-treated, and Being Bored. Fred was the hysterically patriotic commentator.

Another of Jess's favourite sketches involved Ben, Mackenzie and Fred as a girls' band – not playing, just kind of talking to 'camera' about their success. They also finally persuaded Mackenzie to do a sketch as Frodo Baggins – confessing a number of sordid vices to Ricki Lake. Ricki was, of course, played by Jess.

Flora had a running gag as Britney. She would run

randomly on stage – usually while Jess was doing her Miss Thorn impression – and ask if she could take off an item of clothing or shake her ass. Miss Thorn, naturally, sent her off. That one would build, Jess was sure. The audience would be yelling by the end of it.

Of course there was all the organising to do, as well. Ben turned out to be curiously efficient under his laborious, bumbling manner. He booked the school hall for the lunch-hour, the day before school broke up for Christmas, and he persuaded Mr Monroe the sports teacher to do the lighting for them.

One Thursday afternoon Jess and Ben met in the corridor and he showed her the poster design. He'd based it on Flora's parody Great Masters photo of Jess as Girl with a Pearl Nose-ring.

'You really are brilliant at this publicity stuff, Ben,' said Jess.

'I'm – uh – rubbish at acting, though,' said Ben. 'It's really, like, amazing, the way you and Fred can … kind of make up jokes and do imitations of people. And write those scripts together.'

'Yes,' said Jess. 'Sometimes it's like I'm reading his mind. Although often it's totally disgusting.'

'You're a great team,' said Ben.

'Yeah, I'm glad we're back together,' said Jess.

'Hmmm. Kind of tough for the rest of us, though,' said Ben. 'Ah well. I'll get over it. At least I've got the poster.' He waved the artwork of Jess. 'Must remember to – umm, save one for my bedroom wall,' he grinned, and then blushed slightly.

For a moment Jess felt frozen. Was Ben saying … he actually fancied her? Ben Jones, the school love god, whom she had so adored only six months ago?

'Well, gotta go …' mumbled Ben. 'Glad you like the poster. I'll get them printed off tonight.' And he was gone.

Jess stood still for a moment and marvelled at how strange life was. Ben Jones apparently fancied her! Six months ago, the very thought would have made her fall to her knees in shock. But now that she and Fred were together, well, all she felt was a kind of faint nostalgic frisson. The ghost of a thrill. And of course, she felt sorry for Ben. She hoped one day he would find the girl he deserved – somebody wonderful. Although not quite as wonderful as Jess, of course.

Ben, being football captain, was adored by millions, and he got a tribe of small boys to stick the posters up around school. They'd decided to charge a £1 entrance fee and use the show to raise money for charity.

'It's a good idea to do it for charity,' said Flora. 'People will be more tolerant if it's in a good cause.'

'Although let's face it, folks,' said Fred, 'it's not too late to split the takings five ways and run like hell.'

'Shut up, Fred!' said Jess, laughing. They were having a ball, rehearsing. Every spare minute revolved around the show.

One Wednesday morning, Jess ran into Mr Powell in the corridor, and he held up his hand like a policeman, looking rather grim.

'I hear you're going to do a comedy show at the end of term,' said Mr Powell, not looking cross but not looking delighted either.

'Yes, sir.'

'It must be a lot of work.'

'It is.'

'Well, just make sure your homework gets done first,' said Mr Powell with a kind of dark, dangerous scowl. 'Or I'm afraid the show will be cancelled, and that would be a shame after all your efforts.'

He strode off. Jess's knees actually shook with fear. The thought of the show being cancelled made her almost physically sick. She ran off immediately and did some extra homework, even though it hadn't been set, just to be on the safe side.

Of course *Twelfth Night* was going to be the major

event of the term. Jess was afraid that Flora and Fred would both get rather wistful, wishing they'd been involved. The costumes were going to be fabulous, hired from the Royal Shakespeare Company. Jess felt guilty. If it hadn't been for her, Flora and Fred would both be starring in cossies worn by famous actors. Imagine it! Your armpit touching the cloth touched by Ian McKellen's armpit …

'I'm really sorry you're not in *Twelfth Night*, Flo,' she said one night after their rehearsal. The boys had gone home and Jess was staying over at Flora's because it was Friday.

'I don't mind,' said Flora. 'In fact, I've never told you this, but I was really really terrified of being in it. Having such a big part. I was sure I was going to forget my lines or something. The things I do in the comedy show are much better.'

Of course it helped that Jack Stevens and Flora had become An Item. (In record time, incidentally, on their first walk home from the Dolphin Café.) Even Flora's dad approved, because Jack was quite athletic and wanted to go into business when he left school.

'It's a shame Jack and I can't see each other much at the moment because of all our various rehearsals,' said Flora, her eyes sparkling. 'But he's invited me to go skiing with his family in the Christmas hols.'

Jess was thrilled for Flora. It was a match made in heaven. Although privately she was looking forward to a Christmas spent watching horror movies with Fred.

'Promise me,' she said to Fred in one of their rare moments alone together, 'that you will never invite me to go skiing with your family.'

'I can't think of anything more ghastly,' said Fred. 'It combines my two pet hates: physical exercise and cold weather. Don't worry, if we ever get rich we'll give winter sports a miss and buy ourselves a private island in the Caribbean.'

33

YEA, VERILY, THE LION SHALL LIE DOWN WITH THE LAMB BUT DON'T TRY THIS AT HOME

At home things got back to normal after Nori went back to Japan. Mum was a bit quiet for a few days, and there were some long phone calls in the middle of the night. Then one morning Mum made French toast without being asked.

'Lovely, Mum!' said Jess. 'Although I can actually feel it settling on my hips.'

'Sorry I've been a bit preoccupied recently,' said Mum.

'It's OK,' said Jess. 'It's cool. You can go to Tokyo for Christmas if you like. Granny and I will be fine.'

'I wouldn't dream of leaving you alone at Christmas or going to Tokyo!' said Mum. 'It's not an ongoing thing with Nori. It was just – well, a brief encounter.'

'Ah!' said Granny with a sigh. '*Brief Encounter*! That lovely film with Trevor Howard! I wish men wore hats like that nowadays. Those baseball caps are awful. They all look like ducks. And when they wear them back to front it's even worse.'

That night, when Mum came in to kiss Jess goodnight, she looked a little sheepish.

'I'm sorry if I neglected you while I was going out with Nori,' she said.

'No!' said Jess. 'It was fine! I want you to have more brief encounters! I'm sorry I was touchy about it at one stage. But I want you to get out and see people. Men, even. They can be kind of fun. And you haven't had nearly enough boyfriends since you and Dad split up.'

'Haven't I?' said Mum with a sigh. 'How many would be enough, do you think?'

'About three a year,' said Jess. 'Nothing gross. But let's face it, you've been on your own for years and years. I reckon you'll need about fourteen boyfriends a year for the next couple of years, to catch up. That's more than one a month. So get on with it!'

Mum laughed and said goodnight.

For a while Jess couldn't sleep. She thought about Dad. It was time she had a long phone call to him.

She had so much to tell him. She wondered if he had gone to bed yet. She sent him a little text. **HI FAVOURITE MALE PARENT! FANCY A CHAT? OR ARE YOU ALREADY ASLEEP?** She hoped not. It was only 11.15.

Immediately a text came back. **RING ME NOW ON THE LANDLINE. WE'RE STILL UP. WRAPPING PRESENTS. JUST DONE YOURS. IT'S A FUNNY SHAPE.**

Jess got out of bed, tiptoed downstairs, and dialled his number. It was great to hear his voice again.

'So, you absurd small animal of frog-like appearance,' he said, 'how's life treating you?'

'Oh, really great,' said Jess. 'This term has been brilliant. We're doing a comedy show at the end of term. Hey! Could you come? That would be so cool!'

'I'll be there,' said Dad. 'What day is it?'

Once they'd sorted out the date and everything, Dad told her a bit about what he'd been doing. It was a new series of paintings based on ghosts and legends of Cornwall. Jess couldn't wait to see them.

'Maybe you could come down for a few days after Christmas,' said Dad. 'Phil would love to see you again. And bring Fred if you like – if he doesn't mind sleeping on the sofa. No hanky-panky, mind.'

'You're a fine one to talk!' said Jess. 'You're the Prince of Hanky-panky! – Or should I say, the Queen?'

'Sounds like a character in a pantomime,' said Dad. 'So the rehearsals are going well, then? No probs? Everything OK with Fred? I was hoping you'd rung up to cry on my shoulder.'

'Oh, everything's fine now,' said Jess. 'But I did go through a kind of five-star torment at the beginning of term. We've got this new teacher called Miss Thorn who is a beast from the deepest pits of hell.'

Jess told her dad the whole story, including the episode with Ben's shorts, the peeing in the garden with Mr Nishizawa, the visit to the Health Centre whilst wearing no pants, and the whole disgraceful episode of Mr Powell's carpet. Dad laughed quite a lot.

'I can laugh about it now,' said Jess. 'But at the time I was tempted to run away – and come down and live with you in Cornwall. I might just do that anyway.'

'You're welcome any time,' said Dad. 'We need a woman about the house to do all the tiresome chores and disgusting tasks. But everything's all right now, is it? There's nothing bothering you?'

'Well, there is just one little niggling thing,' said Jess. She hadn't really been completely aware of it, but talking to Dad like this now had kind of brought it to the surface, and she realised it had been bothering her, in a buried way, for some time.

'In the show I do this – well, I'm kind of the link presenter among other things, and I do it as Miss Thorn.'

'The beast from the deepest pits of hell?'

'The very same,' said Jess. 'The trouble is, it's really great, the script works fine, I'm just … well, I suppose I'm just a tiny bit scared that she'll react badly.'

'You haven't used her real name?'

'No, in the show she's called Susie Sunbeam.'

Dad laughed. This was promising.

'I'm sure she'll be OK about it,' said Dad. 'If she got upset she'd just look a fool. But if she does get mad, you can come and live with me.'

'Fantastic! But, Dad, can I bring Mum and Granny and Fred as well?' said Jess.

'Nothing would please me more,' said Dad. 'But obviously, Fred would have to live outdoors until you were engaged.'

'It's OK,' said Jess. 'We can tie him to the railings. It would only be for about five years.'

They laughed. But deep down inside, Jess remained just ever so slightly terrified of Miss Thorn's reaction to being lampooned, and hoped that, on the morning of the show, Miss Thorn would have the decency to break a leg and be whisked off by an air ambulance.

34

BLESSED ARE THE
PISS-TAKERS

Jess thought today's Biblical proverb must be Dad's way of wishing her luck in the show. Although he was actually going to be there in person, which was ace. She'd asked permission for Dad and Phil to come and that was OK, especially as Phil was providing a lot of the costumes and all the wigs, and helping with the quick costume changes – he used to be a stage designer and was bringing loads of clothes from his boutique.

Tickets sold like hot cakes. They sold so many they had to print more. And contrary to Jess's expectations, teachers bought them as well. The day came. The hall was packed. Jess was all ready, waiting in the wings in her Miss Thorn costume. They had borrowed a power suit from Flora's mum, and Phil had fixed Jess's hair so it looked just like Miss Thorn's.

Jess herself had designed her scary, flaring eyebrows. But despite her terrifying appearance, she herself had never felt so nervous in her life.

'Oh my God!' whispered Flora, joining Jess backstage in her Britney outfit. 'You made me jump! I thought you were actually her for a moment!'

'They're all there!' Mackenzie was peeping through the curtains. 'All the teachers and everything. Irritable Powell, Thorn, the lot.'

Jess felt a terrible stab of panic. She had sort of known Miss Thorn would actually be here, but she hadn't anticipated just how frightening it would be.

The excited hubbub was hushed as the lights dimmed. Jess's heart was racing. She had to walk out now as Miss Thorn with Miss Thorn watching! She took a deep breath and walked out into the spotlight.

There was uproar. Pandemonium. People actually shrieked with shocked, ecstatic laughter. Jess raked the auditorium with a snooty stare. She rubbed her thumb against her index finger, just like Miss Thorn did. She glared at the audience, flaring the whites of her eyes. She pursed her lips. Then she raised her hand. A hush fell, punctuated by scattered giggles.

'Be quiet!' she snapped. 'You haven't come here to enjoy yourselves.' They howled. Jess waited, hands on hips, the way Miss Thorn stood when she was rattled. Eventually the audience fell silent. They so much wanted to hear her speak again.

'My name,' said Jess in Miss Thorn's high, whiny voice, 'is Susie Sunbeam. Cross me at your peril.'

More laughs. Jess began to wonder if they would ever get to the first sketch. It was a dream start.

Eventually the first sketch unfolded: the girl group talking to camera about their success. Fred, Mackenzie and Ben in big hair and miniskirts, sitting kind of scrunched up together on a sofa. (The sole piece of furniture on the set, incidentally – borrowed from Flora's granny, who had so many sofas there was a rumour she was breeding them.)

At the sight of the boys dressed as a girly band, the audience fell about. Then they launched into their high-pitched American accents.

'We really hit the big tahm aftah we played the Fruit Bowl in Sacramenno,' drawled Fred.

'Like, we becayme rowl mahdels,' added Mackenzie. 'Plus I wuz voted the girl with the cutest ass by *Music* magazine.'

'Show 'em yo' ass, Shirlene,' said Ben, flicking his long blonde wig out of his eyes.

'No, I won't, Barbie,' said Mackenzie. ''Cause this is a family show. Oh, OK.' He got up and whirled around, lifting his miniskirt to give the audience an eyeful of gold lame hot-pants of the sort made popular by endless MTV videos.

Halfway through the sketch, Flora ran on as Britney. She was instantly recognised by the audience, who cheered. For once in Jess's life, she was glad Flora looked so much like the Queen of Pop.

'C'n I take my top off now?' called Britney.

The other 'girls' got up in indignation and shooed her off. '*Get outta here, Britney! This is our show. We gonna scratch yo' eyes out if you say one mo' word!*' Flora ran off again.

The girly band then mimed to a Sugababes number. The audience loved it. They clapped and cheered as the girly band made their bow. Then it was Jess's turn again. She strode on to the stage and turned to the audience with a terrifying white-eyed glare.

'Be quiet!' she snapped. 'Wipe that smile off your face, Smith. Nobody's amused.' The audience erupted. 'Some of you seem to think you can do what you like in here,' she went on. 'You at the back, stop laughing! And see me afterwards.

'Now, as I was saying, my name is Susie Sunbeam. It has a pleasing alliteration, as you can appreciate. Alliteration is when a Christian name and a surname begin with the same letter. As in Mike Myers. Or

Freddie Flintstone.'

'Or Jess Jordan!' shouted someone in the audience. Jess flinched. Everybody laughed.

'Don't even think of mentioning that name!' hissed Jess. 'Despite its alliteration, it has a very unpleasant sound. I would never trust a person with a name like that. It sounds somehow frightfully common.' Everybody roared. She had departed from her script, but she had to get back on course. The gang had had enough time for their quick change – off with the wigs and miniskirts, on with the sports shorts.

'And now – sit still when I'm talking!' More laughter. 'We are going to study a phenomenon which dates from classical times. The Olympics. The challenge is to apply Olympic principles to everyday life. And now over to our commentator Reg Filbert at The Pointless Olympics.'

She backed offstage, there was a brassy fanfare of heroic Olympics-type music, and Fred walked on holding a microphone and with one finger in his ear.

'Thank you, Susie,' he said. 'The rather disappointing news for Team GB is that plucky Andy Kerbstone has had to pull out of the sandwich-making with a sore big toe. But we're able to bring you the main event of the evening: Picking the Nose Whilst Standing on One Leg.'

Ben, Mackenzie and Flora all walked on in sports gear, doing various warming-up exercises and looking heroic and motivated.

'On your marks, get set, go!' shouted Phil, firing a starting pistol offstage. Immediately they all stood on one leg and started picking their noses.

'Two things matter here,' said Fred, in a hushed excited tone. 'Obviously, the athletes have to stand on one leg – the British Representative Harriet Podge has been training down at Walford Harriers, out in all weathers for years, standing on one leg for half an hour before most of us are even out of bed. That's what I call dedication.'

Flora lost her balance and toppled to the ground. 'Oh no!' cried Fred. 'The plucky British girl has gone! She lost it coming up to the half-minute mark! Now it's between the Croatian and the Greek!'

Ben picked his nose and pretended to flick a bit across the stage.

'And that's a massive flick from the Croatian!' said Fred. 'It's absolutely huge! It's over fifteen feet! That's his personal best and a new World Record!'

The Pointless Olympics went down a storm. The audience particularly liked Trying Not to Cry Whilst Thinking of Puppies Being Ill-treated.

Then, after the Olympics came a great little Ricki

Lake interview in which Mackenzie as Frodo Baggins owned up to a history of domestic violence, and Gandalf (played by Fred in a long white beard and pointy hat) admitted to chocolate addiction and several centuries of shoplifting from Woolworth's.

Then there was a sketch in which Flora and Ben tried to plan a demo protesting about the negative image of blondes in society, but their ability to organise it was hampered by their lack of brain cells.

'We'll … uh, have to have it outdoors, yeah?' pondered Ben.

'Er,' said Flora, frowning in an empty-headed manner, 'what's … *outdoors* mean, exactly?'

Jess and Fred were watching from the wings. 'Nice little piece of typecasting there,' whispered Fred, and in the darkness he put his arm around Jess and hugged her. 'Feels kind of pervy hugging Miss Thorn,' he went on. 'I could really get into it.'

The blondes sketch ended, and Jess strode out into the spotlight again. She was greeted by an enormous cheer. She held up a hand. Silence. The feeling of power was amazing. But it was the power of comedy, not the power of fear.

'Quiet!' she barked. 'We're coming to the end of this entertainment now, and some of you have behaved so badly that there's going to be a special detention after school.'

Here Flora ran on again as Britney. The audience cheered for her too. They loved these running gags.

'Can I take my top off now?' asked Flora.

'*YES!*' yelled the audience. Jess whirled round to them, flaring the whites of her eyes and raking them with her laser-like glance.

'Some of you appear to think that this is amusing!' she snapped. 'I can assure you, there's absolutely nothing to laugh about. And no, Spears, you may not remove your clothing. Go away and get on with your essay on The Importance of Modesty.'

Flora ran off, to more cheers. Jess held up her hand.

'And now,' she said, 'pray silence for the school song, which has been re-written in honour of a very important guest.' Jess was joined by Fred, Ben and Flora, and they performed the words of the school song to the tune of God Save the Queen. At the very end Mackenzie walked on dressed as the Queen and did a bit of stilted royal waving as the audience applauded, cheered, and drummed on the floor with their feet. Then the house lights went up. Mr Powell, who had been sitting at the front, stood up.

'I'm sure you'd all like me to congratulate Jess, Flora, Fred, Mackenzie and Ben,' he said. 'This was a terrific show, and they've raised almost £1,000 for the Teenage Cancer Trust.' More cheers. 'What's more,' said Mr Powell, 'their timing has been perfect. In a minute the bell's going to go for afternoon school – so will you please file out in an orderly manner and go to your classrooms for registration.'

How very dull that sounded after all the comedy. Jess and the gang trooped off and began to unwind in the dressing room backstage.

'It was fabulous!' said Phil. Dad gave Jess a big hug, then got busy collecting the costumes and helping Phil put the wigs carefully back into the boxes.

Despite Mr Powell's instructions that everybody should go to registration, the dressing room immediately began to fill up with people congratulating them.

'It was fantastic!' said Jodie, hugging Jess. 'You're a genius! So much more fun than *Twelfth Night*!'

'Oh, don't be hard on Shakespeare,' said Jess. '*Twelfth Night* has been fun for nearly five hundred years, which ain't bad.'

'Miss Thorn was really cracking up!' said Tom. 'Every time you appeared as her, she covered her face and, like, cringed!'

'Really?' said Jess. She felt the cold spear of anxiety again. Despite Tom's report that Miss Thorn had been laughing, Jess would ideally not wish to see her again as long as she lived. Then Jodie looked up and went pale.

'Watch out,' she murmured, 'here she comes.'

Jess looked round and there was Miss Thorn, coming through the crowd towards her. Sheer terror gripped Jess's soul. But, oh joy! Mr Fothergill was with her – walking with a stick, but looking really happy to be back after his accident. He reached Jess first.

'Congratulations, Jess!' he said. 'That was absolutely first-rate. I've been telling Miss Thorn that you've always been my star pupil as regards comedy.'

Miss Thorn looked uneasy. She was avoiding Jess's eye. Jess's heart was racing. But Mr Fothergill just went burbling on, bless him.

'I was particularly impressed with your mimicry. I don't know which I enjoyed more: your Ricki Lake or your Miss Thorn. Do you think Jess did you justice?' He turned to Miss Thorn and smiled. Miss Thorn flinched slightly and gave a thin, grudging smile.

'It's rather unnerving to see oneself on stage, of course,' said Miss Thorn. 'But I have to admit I did recognise a few of my own irritating mannerisms.'

'It's lucky Miss Thorn is such a good sport!' beamed Mr Fothergill. Jess wasn't sure Miss Thorn would have been quite so sporting if Mr Fothergill hadn't been standing beside her, radiating bonhomie.

'Yes, thanks for being OK about it,' said Jess graciously. Miss Thorn gave another unconvincing twitchy smile.

'Well, I must go and congratulate the others,' she said, and moved away. Mr Fothergill stayed, beaming at Jess and looking like a happy pig.

'Are you coming back next term, Mr Fothergill?' asked Jess. 'We've really missed you.'

'Yes, I'll be back next term,' he said. 'I've made a good recovery and I can't wait.'

'Is Miss Thorn … leaving, then?'

'Oh yes,' said Mr Fothergill. 'She was just covering for me this term.'

'Phew!' said Jess. She couldn't help heaving a little sigh of relief. 'She was really nice to me just now, but usually she's, well – she's terrifying.'

'You know why that is?' said Mr Fothergill. 'It's because *she* is scared witless of *you*.'

'Of me? No, no, that can't be right.'

'Of all of you,' said Mr Fothergill. 'She was telling me earlier. It's her first job, and she was so terrified, she was sick every morning for the first week.'

Good Lord above! Who would have thought it? So, Miss Thorn, herself personally responsible for an outbreak of Fear and Loathing at Ashcroft School, was secretly as scared as hell.

Eventually the crowd thinned. Mr Powell appeared briefly and told them they had done so well they could go home early. Dad and Phil had already left, taking the costumes. They had a supper date with Jess and Fred that night at a Chinese restaurant.

Jess leant back and let out a long, long sigh of relief. Fred came and sat by her while she put her socks and shoes on.

'The verdict seems to be that we were simply brilliant,' said Fred. 'Hey, guys!' He turned to Flora, Mackenzie and Ben. 'I want to give credit where it's due – thanks to Jess, without whom this would never have happened. Lady and gentlemen, she took four nerds and transformed us with her genius into fabulous stars of stage and screen – well, stage anyway, at least for the present. Friends, I give you – Jess Jordan!'

They cheered, and Fred leant over and placed a kiss on her cheek. It was the first time he had ever kissed her in public. A sparkling thrill ran up Jess's spine, like liquid tinsel.

'And now,' said Fred, 'we ought to start planning our show for the Edinburgh Festival next year.'

They strolled off out of the dressing room and

down the corridor. Fred and Jess went on ahead; Ben, Flora and Mackenzie followed, joking and relaxing. They walked through the reception area, past gangs of adoring little kids, and out into the fresh air.

Fred put his arm around Jess's shoulders. 'I'm proud to be seen with you now,' he said. 'Obviously, public caresses were out of the question while you were a loser wearing no pants. But now you have become a terrifying success I think I might hang on to you for dear life.'

'Public caresses were also out of the question whilst you were being a complete wuss,' said Jess. 'Now you're a successful producer and director I might just tolerate your presence. But don't push your luck, Parsons. Don't turn into a doting freak. You can go off a person just like that, you know.'

She grinned at him. This was one of the really great moments. Suddenly, something spiralled down out of the sky and landed on Fred's hair. A snowflake!

'It's snowing!' cried Jess. 'How immensely cool!'

'Quite literally!' agreed Fred, putting his tongue out and catching the next snowflake. They ate snow for a while, and then they began to feel the need for something a little more filling.

'Hold my hand,' said Fred. 'It'll be good practice for when I'm ninety.' His hand felt extra warm in the cold Christmassy air. Fairy lights twinkled on the tree beside the school gate and, across the road, an obese halogen Santa waved menacingly at them from the roof of the supermarket.

As they walked out through the school gates, Jess saw the low wall where she had sat, waiting in vain for Fred during their first major misunderstanding. That was six months ago.

So much had happened in six months! Certain mysteries had been unravelled: her dad's exotic life down in St Ives, and the reason why her parents had separated. There had been real progress on every front.

Grandpa's ashes had been scattered on the sea, so he was laid to rest. His soul was probably even now frolicking with mermaids – if that sort of thing was permitted in the afterlife. So Granny could stop fretting and devote her whole attention to homicide.

Mum had become more confident, and after years of mere gardening, had actually had a relationship with a man – a glamorous Japanese toyboy, no less. There was still work to be done on Mum's wardrobe, however. Jess was planning a maternal makeover in which her mum's charity shop hobo coat was replaced by an Armani suit.

As for Jess herself … she had come a long way

since midsummer. She'd realised that her feelings for Ben Jones had just been a crush. She'd refused to be intimidated by Miss Thorn. She'd found a way of standing up for herself through – rather appropriately – stand-up comedy.

But best of all, she'd got together with Fred. Jess knew she was never going to go off him. And in future, if they had any more major misunderstandings, she was sure they'd be able to sort them out. They'd talk. They'd hug. And if things got really bad, she was prepared to put Fred in his place with a swift kick in the teeth.

Life was just about perfect. OK, she was a tad overweight. But she would sort that out in a couple of weeks via a New Year's Resolution. But right now …

'Dolphin Café?' asked Fred. Jess nodded and squeezed his hand.

It was a bit too early to walk into the sunset, so they just strolled off happily down the road, towards the smell of doughnuts.